A *Dire Wolves* MISSION

Savage Sacrifice

A *Dire Wolves* MISSION

ELLIS LEIGH

Kinship Press

Savage Sacrifice: A Dire Wolves Mission

First Edition

ISBN
978-1-944336-20-2

Kinship Press
P.O. Box 221
Prospect Heights, IL 60070

He who envies others does not obtain peace of mind.

— BUDDHA

One

*O*nce upon a time, the sounds a couple made while having sex didn't bother Phego. In fact, if he searched his memory hard and deep, he'd probably find moments where he rather enjoyed listening in. The soft grunts, the slap of skin on skin, the growl as an Alpha wolf in human form took what was being given to him. There was a rhythm to it, a draw and pulse that appealed. At least, there had been. Once or twice…many, many years ago.

Not on that day.

Because on that day, the banging, slamming, and yelling—the almost violent sounds of two people fucking—haunted him like a bad dream. There had never been a moment in his life Phego had wanted to cut off his own ears more. But that seemed painful and excessive, even for him, so he took off for his favorite spot instead. Looking to escape the symphony of sin and lust before he did something stupid like scream at his neighbors to shut the fuck up.

When Phego had offered the newly mated couple the

chance to move in to the old, neglected cabin at the back of his property, he hadn't expected to spend so much time hiding in the woods along the valley floor. The scenery was beautiful, almost pristine in its lack of human influence. But that wasn't why he picked it to hole up in. Not the main reason, at least. Mostly he ran to that particular spot because it was far enough away not to have to overhear Thaus and Ariel mating. Again. And again.

Over the past few months, he'd gotten good at identifying the lead-up. It took little more than a giggle or sigh for Phego to pay attention; a single grunt or whispered curse for him to shift and head down the mountain. If anyone had asked him why, he'd have said he was giving the couple their privacy. Truth be told, Phego had grown up in wolf packs. There was no such thing as privacy with ears that picked up every sigh, noses that could scent a woman's arousal from a hundred yards away, and the keen animal sight that had kept him alive so long. No, privacy was an illusion. What he was doing at the bottom of the mountain was saving himself from the agonizing sense of yearning whenever he heard those two together.

Yearning for something he couldn't have and didn't want.

He gave the couple almost two hours to get their lust and desire out of their system before heading back up the hill toward his own cabin, the empty one. The itch of an unfulfilled need tortured him on the way home—as it always did when he'd spent time hiding. The ache of something needed nipping at his heels the entire trip. Both were feelings he'd eventually wrap his fingers around...and strangle.

There was no time for such ridiculousness, no sense in craving things you couldn't have. He had a job to do, a breed to protect, and a newly mated couple to help keep safe. Besides, he wouldn't have allowed a mate into his life, even if one did somehow magically show up. Let his brothers deal with all that; he'd never trust a strange woman to get so close to him. How could he? It'd taken him centuries to truly have faith in his brothers, his pack. No shewolf would stick around and wait for him to grow comfortable with her. It would be a wasted effort on the fates' part even to offer him the option.

But knowledge didn't quench his thirst for something he didn't have. A fact that made his blood boil and his mind spin with dark, angry thoughts. He needed to tuck those away, though. Ariel would sense his mood in a second if she saw him, and he didn't want to upset her. She was a woman he'd almost instantly trusted, one he befriended easily. An anomaly in his life, and one that caused him great stress. It wasn't until he'd accepted Ariel so easily that he'd begun to think of his own possible mate. Of the chance that maybe…maybe.

He shut that thought down quick. No chance, no mate, no trusting random shewolves. Period.

As Phego approached his cabin, as he worked to settle his thoughts and calm his mind, he thrashed and pounded through the brush so the couple could hear him coming. Just in case. He wouldn't head to their place, but at least he'd given them a warning that he was back in the area. Maybe if they heard *him*, they'd realize he could hear *them*. That hadn't happened yet, but he hoped. He hoped every single day.

But instead of sleepy breathing, soft sighs, or the flat-out collisions of flesh from another round of fucking, what he heard was the sound of Ariel crying coming from the little cabin in the woods. He was on their porch in seconds, shifting to his human form and yanking on a spare pair of shorts before he could even take a breath.

"What is it?" he asked as soon as he opened the door. He hadn't even knocked, something Thaus would certainly understand, though. When it came to Ariel's safety, there was only one rule. Do whatever it takes.

"Hey, Phego." Ariel tried to smile, but her eyes were red and her face puffy. She'd been crying for a while.

No threat, no intruders, no sign of danger. And yet, Ariel cried. Phego couldn't put the pieces together. "What's going on? Where's Thaus?"

The man walked out of the back bedroom as if summoned. Phego blinked, unable to tie the sad, sorry-looking being with the shifter he knew Thaus to be. Shoulders slumped, head tipped forward as if submitting, Thaus stood with a hangdog look on his face Phego had never seen before. Phego couldn't fathom what had happened in the few hours he'd been gone, couldn't imagine what could upset the couple so horribly. At least, not until Thaus dropped his black mission bag at his feet.

"Shit," hissed Phego, wanting so badly to reach out and grab Ariel's arm. To hold her up as she swayed slightly in her fear and grief. "Can I go in your place?"

Thaus shook his head, unable to tear his eyes away from his mate for more than a second at a time. "It's explosives trading revolving around a direct threat to Blaze. Luc feels I'm the only one who could pick up code words or patterns if they're selling, and he's worried what a slip might mean for the entire shifter population should that occur. He wants me on this mission."

The urge to say fuck Luc was strong, but it wasn't something Phego could do in good conscience. If Luc—their leader and pack Alpha—needed Thaus on a mission, there was a damn good reason. And protecting Blaze—the president of the National Association of the Lycan Brotherhood, the ruling power of all wolf shifters in North America—was a damn good reason. In fact, he was just about the only reason other than another Dire Wolf in jeopardy that would override all other policies and procedures for the pack. While the other Dires knew enough about explosive devices to get by, even

Phego had to admit Thaus possessed the most knowledge of the bunch in that arena. The entire team relied on Thaus in moments where explosives were needed or feared, including Luc. Their intrepid leader wouldn't pull a mated pair apart when there were other options, especially not considering Ariel's condition.

As Phego watched, Ariel's hand slipped down to her belly. Rubbing her *condition* in an almost unconscious way.

"It'll be fine," she said, standing tall and trying so hard to be brave, even though he knew Thaus could see right through her. Just as he did. "We'll be fine. I'm just spoiled since you haven't had a mission outside of protecting me in all these months." She swallowed hard, her eyes filling again, her lips twisting as she fought back some emotion that looked painful. "When do you think you'll be back?"

Thaus growled and hurried to kneel in front of her, resting his forehead against the baby bump that had been slowly growing over the past few months. "Soon. I promise you. I won't be able to call, but I'll make sure to be here before this little wolf is born. I swear I'll make it back."

"I know you will." But even as Ariel said the words, she was looking at him with flat, almost disconnected eyes. Doubting his ability to keep that promise. Phego had gone on two missions since the one that rescued her, and both times his timeline had gotten completely fucked by unforeseen circumstances. Her view of their missions was one of lengthy absences and missed deadlines, so of course she doubted her mate. But her baby was coming, whether Thaus was there or not. A fact that couldn't be denied. This was the most horrible timing for a mission Phego had ever seen.

"I'm sorry," Thaus whispered, clinging to her hips. "If there was any way I could get out of it—"

"I know," Ariel replied as she ran her fingers over his

shorn head. "You've got six weeks until the birth. Plenty of time to go save the shifter world. We'll be here, waiting."

Thaus kissed her belly and gave her hip a squeeze before climbing to his feet once more. The sad puppy look was gone, replaced by one of fierce determination and downright rage. Thaus was back. "Phego, I'm going to need you to look after my life for me."

Phego's response was easy, almost instinct. "Done."

"I don't want her left alone."

"Understood."

Thaus tore his gaze from Ariel's face, giving Phego a stern yet pleading look. "I know this is a lot to ask, but I'd like it if you'd move in here while I'm gone. Ariel will be more comfortable in her own home, and she needs someone with her all the time. I don't want to risk her or the baby."

Phego darted a look to the shewolf, who seemed almost relieved at the idea. Fuck. He liked Ariel, liked her a lot, but living in the same house with her would probably test his patience in ways he wasn't even aware of yet. He was very used to his solitude, his quiet times in his own den.

But it was Thaus asking and Ariel agreeing to the idea. Phego might be able to turn down one, but he'd never be able to argue against both. Especially not if Ariel kept looking at him as if he was about to save her somehow. She was a weakness to his strength, a sliver keeping him from closing himself off to people. He'd been amazed by the spunk and grit of the little Omega shewolf since he met her. Her bravery and strength belied her small stature, though, and her huge, loving heart welcomed even an asshole like him. He trusted her more than any of the other Dire Wolf mates that had come along in recent years. Trusted her more than anyone other than his Dire brothers, for sure. Phego would just have to get over his aversion to having people around— for Thaus. For Ariel.

"Done," Phego said, making sure his response was strong and sure for their sake. "I can take one of the attic rooms."

"You don't have to do this," Ariel said, but the way her shoulders had relaxed the second he'd agreed was enough for Phego to know her words were a lie.

"Yes, I do. It'll be fine."

"Good. Done." Thaus grabbed his phone and tucked it into a pocket in his mission bag. "Phego moves in, I go save a pack from some really bad guys before they make the world go boom, Ariel sits tight and doesn't do anything that could bring on early labor."

The shewolf rubbed her belly again, a sure sign of her nerves. "Not happening. No Thaus, no baby. I'm making that a rule. We're a team."

Phego felt the conviction behind her words, could practically see the connection between them. The love and trust and faith they had in one another. And for one brief moment, he coveted it. For a single second before he locked that door in his mind tight.

"Mine," Thaus growled as he moved in and nuzzled into her neck. "All mine."

Something Phego knew he'd never say about another person.

But the light mood of the good-bye changed in an instant, grew heavy and dark. Sad even as Ariel whispered, "Come back soon to me."

"Promise," Thaus said, matching her somber tone.

Phego stepped back, tucking himself into the entrance to the kitchen, giving the couple another illusion of privacy. This would be hard on both of them; hell, it would be hard on Phego as well. But he'd signed up to be their protector, had volunteered his woods and extra cabin to keep them close. Dealing with a lonely shewolf pining for her mate was part of his life for the moment, and he'd make sure he did a damn good job taking care of her.

Thaus growled low, squeezing his mate as close as he could with all that baby in the way. "I swear I will find a way to get back in time. No matter what."

Thaus looked over her shoulder and right at Phego, making his point clear. Making his doubts clear. Phego nodded, knowing he and Deus would have to work together to help Thaus from afar. The tech god that was Dire Wolf Deus would know what to do and how to manage monitoring a covert operation for sure, and Phego would be ready to roll out in Thaus' place should the need occur. Thaus would be at his baby's birth. Phego would make sure of it.

"Okay." Ariel eventually nodded against Thaus' chest and took a deep breath before pulling out of his grip. "I think I'll call in Michaela a little early."

Phego growled, unable to hold it back as she threw a wrench into his plans to keep her safe. "Who's this Michaela guy, and why is he being called at all?"

Thaus frowned. "Michaela is a woman, a shewolf Ariel knows from her med school days. She's also a midwife and will be delivering the little angel my mate's carrying."

"And you think this is a good idea? Bringing in strangers when I'm the only one here to protect her?"

"I trust Michaela," Ariel said, looking determined and sure. Phego had learned early on that there was no pushing her once she got that look. She'd simply set her heels and refuse to budge if you tried. He'd need to be cautious.

"You may trust her, but I don't know her. You and the baby are mine to guard while Thaus is away. It would make my life easier if I didn't have to be watching an extra wolf who may or may not be here for the right reasons."

Ariel crossed her arms over her chest. "And if the baby comes? Are you going to crawl between my legs to help me? Are you going to put your hand inside of me to check the progress?"

Thaus' growl shook the windows, his eyes swirling silver as his wolf pushed forward. "Phego—"

"No." Phego held his hands up and took three steps back, giving the wolf time to settle. "I would do whatever I could to keep you safe, but Thaus would skin me alive if I tried any of that."

"Exactly. So Michaela's coming. Don't worry—you'll like her. She's amazing."

Amazing. Right. Phego hated the thought of a stranger in his woods, but Ariel was right. She'd need someone to help her through the delivery whether Thaus was back in time or not. Thaus would have understood if Phego had needed to deliver the baby, but it would have altered their relationship for sure. A mated wolf would never want another male anywhere near his shewolf's pussy, even if it was for medical care. That was instinct, plain and simple.

So Phego would move in with Ariel, and he would allow this stranger to come live in the cabin in the woods with them. *And* he would keep his eyes on Ariel every second of the day. She may have trusted this person, but he didn't. He didn't trust anyone outside his pack brothers and maybe their mates. Maybe.

"Stay safe," Thaus said as he kissed Ariel on the forehead. The move was so sweet, so intimate in a nonsexual way, that Phego couldn't watch.

"Come back to me," she whispered. There were low growls and the sounds of good-bye kisses, but Phego didn't look. Didn't even attempt to sneak a peek at their affection. This should have been private time for the couple, and he hated being any sort of witness to such things.

"I have to go." Thaus coughed, which made Phego turn. "I'll walk you back to your place so you can grab your stuff to make the move."

Phego knew that was a lie to get him alone, and by the

look on Ariel's face, so did she. But she was a good mate and a smart woman—she kept her mouth shut and let Thaus think he was getting away with something.

Phego followed Thaus out the door and down the porch steps. Neither spoke until they'd circled to the far side of Phego's house, gotten far enough away that Ariel might not hear what he had to say. Might not, but Phego knew she'd be listening.

"I don't know this Michaela," Thaus said, looking more torn than Phego had ever seen him. "I'm trying to be the supportive mate the women keep telling me I need to be, but—"

"But the idea of a stranger around your very pregnant mate while you're not here to keep an eye on things makes you want to blow up the road leading to our woods so they can't reach her."

Thaus stared, his face dark, his eyes swirling. "Exactly."

Cool. They were on the same page, then. "I've got your back. She won't be left alone with Ariel."

"I know it's a lot—"

"I owe you." And he did. Phego owed Thaus his life. This, in comparison to what the shifter had done for him? It was nothing.

Thaus ran a hand over his head, looking back the way they'd come. "Normally, I'd tell you that debt was paid. But this time—"

"That debt will never be paid, and there's no need to explain. Ariel is the most important thing in your world. Pregnant Ariel ratchets that up to about a level fifteen."

Thaus growled. "Twenty."

"Fine. Twenty. I get it." Phego waited until he had the Dire's full attention before placing his hand over his heart and looking him right in the eye. "You saved my life when you didn't have to. You didn't even know me, and you certainly didn't know the situation you walked into, but you saved me anyway. I will never be able to repay you. Taking care of your mate and unborn child is barely a start."

"If anything happens to them—"

"It won't. On my honor. I'd lay down my life for them."

Thaus nodded, still looking grim. "I'll kill Luc if I miss the birth."

"So don't. Get your shit done and haul ass back here."

"That's the plan." He grabbed Phego's forearm, pulling him in close. "Keep them safe."

"On my word."

Thaus trudged over to his Harley, the one he kept parked in Phego's carport as the path to his own cabin was too rough for the bike. He was about to climb on when Ariel yelled his name and came running through the trees. Thaus snapped around and moved, closing the distance between them in three easy steps before pulling her off her feet and into his arms.

"I needed one more good-bye," she said, clinging to him.

"I was going to ride back up to the cabin, baby," Thaus said. "Besides, no good-byes. Not ever. This is just a see you in a few."

She pulled back, giving him a watery smile. "See you in a few, then."

Thaus growled and held her tighter, pressing his lips to her forehead. "Stay with Phego."

"I will."

Phego stepped beside her as Thaus set her on her feet, worried about the strain of saying good-bye to her mate and how it would affect the baby. Thaus and Ariel hadn't been separated for more than a couple of hours since they'd mated, hadn't been apart for anywhere near as long as they were about to be in all that time. This was new, and Phego was ready for any reaction from his strong but hormonal ward.

When Thaus moved to climb onto his bike that time, nothing stopped him. He gave a hearty wave before starting the engine and turning for the road, riding like hell as if going slow wouldn't be enough to pull him away. The Dire needed speed to go, needed strength. Even without a mate, Phego understood that.

Ariel stood at Phego's side, both of them watching the taillights disappear down the treelined trail that led to the main road. Her fighting not to cry, him in tune with every breath and twitch just in case. She shook with the power of her emotions, but she held herself together. Phego knew that wouldn't last—that she'd break at some point—but the fact that she was able to hold herself together at all was pretty impressive. Such a strong wolf shifter.

When Thaus was gone, when the lights were no longer visible, and even the roar of the engine had faded with the distance, Ariel sighed. "Guess I'll go call Michaela."

Phego grunted, still hating the idea of strangers in his woods. "I should pack a bag."

"I'll make us a nice dinner. Might as well start this roommate thing off right." Her smile was watery but there, her shoulders back and strong. Yeah, she'd break soon. Not yet, though. And probably not in front of him.

Phego pretended not to notice the way her shoulders shook, or how red her eyes were getting. Instead, he nodded and headed inside as she picked her way along the path to her own cabin. She needed time to process, but he couldn't afford to give her much. Three minutes…that was all the time he felt comfortable leaving her alone, which meant he needed to hurry. Before she was out of sight, he was loading his own mission bag for the weeks ahead. Explosives, handguns, rifles, ammunition, listening devices…the usual.

Ariel could trust Michaela to the moon and back, but Phego knew better. He didn't trust anyone beyond his own Dire brothers, and even that had taken centuries to earn. Without Thaus at his side, he never would have stuck around the pack long enough to fit in. But Thaus and Luc had saved him when he'd been betrayed by the ones who should have had his back, so they'd earned his loyalty. A tough feat to be sure.

Ariel was smart and savvy when it came to the people she surrounded herself with. She'd experienced firsthand the evils lurking within strangers, but she hadn't ever had her pack turn on her. Hadn't had her own parents try to murder her. Hadn't been sold out by her only blood sibling.

No, for as much darkness as Ariel had seen, she was still clinging to the light. That made her special. Phego had long since given up such things. He lived in the darkness, luxuriated in it. He never thought the best of people, and he certainly wouldn't start with this midwife.

Michaela could come into his woods, but she wouldn't be welcomed by him. In fact, as Phego grabbed some clothes and tossed them on top of his portable armory, he did what any good Dire Wolf would do in his situation. He shot a text to Deus.

Possible enemy invited inside. Ready the eyes and ears on the ground. Be prepared to move on target.

It took less than ten seconds to get a reply.

Force level?

Phego didn't even have to think about that one.

Kill at first sign of threat.

He shouldered his bag and headed out the door. It was mission time.

_M_ichaela wasn't sure at what point in her life her Alpha had decided she didn't have the right to make her own decisions, but it certainly seemed as if that had become an issue.

"I'm going." She raised her chin and crossed her arms over her chest, daring him to argue. Which he did.

"Not without protection." Her Alpha glared, responding to her frown with one of his own, along with a widening of his stance. Some sort of dominance move, for sure. But Michaela could play that same game.

She mimicked his body language, placing her hands on her hips for good measure. "I don't need a bodyguard."

"No bodyguard, no trip."

Michaela growled, unable to hold it back. "But they're expecting me. This is my friend, my Omega sister. She wouldn't have called me away from my pack if it wasn't vital. She needs my help, and I refuse to turn my back on her."

Her Alpha shook his head, not looking the least bit

sorry. "The danger to the Omegas is not over. The threat against you is not gone. You can go to help your friend, but you have to take one of my enforcers with you."

Michaela stared him down, hoping he'd break, knowing by the firm stare on his face that he never would. His mind was made up. Her only hope was for some sort of compromise. One inkling of control.

"Which one?" she asked, narrowing her eyes at the man who held her pack's fate in his hands. He may have been the boss, but she'd been around this block a few times. Bodyguards, shadows, enforcers—half her life had been spent being watched over. The least he could do was give her the opportunity to pick her poison.

Her Alpha's eyes flickered, the first flash of doubt the man had shown in the weeks she'd been fighting for his permission to take the trip. "Colt."

Oh, hell.

"No. Not Colt. He's too…rough. He'll scare my patient." She didn't say that he'd also probably pick a fight with her patient's mate. Colt wasn't exactly easy on other males, and Michaela refused to be a source of stress for the new couple. Especially seeing as she hadn't met the male yet.

When Michaela had received the call that the friend she hadn't heard from in close to a year had found her fated mate, she'd been slightly jealous. Any shewolf would be, really. And when the woman she thought of as a sister had said she was pregnant—that she needed someone to help with the delivery, that she couldn't trust anyone other than Michaela—that jealousy had turned to something much more like relief. At least Michaela knew her place in her pack. She trusted them with everything, had fought beside them when the need arose. She'd never doubted her pack would take care of her.

That didn't mean her Alpha didn't piss her off something

fierce now and again. Like when he assigned her Colt of all people as a babysitter. He knew exactly how hard Colt could be on others, knew how uncomfortable he made her. This was a test to see if she was truly committed to going. One she needed to pass.

"Look. I'll take a bodyguard if it'll make you feel better, but not Colt. Anyone but him. Assign someone else, and I'll agree to your demands without another word."

Her Alpha stared hard, his mind obviously made up, his determination unbreakable as she gave away the chink in her own armor. "He's the only one I trust. I want you safe, Michaela. I want you to return to us in one piece." He reached for her, his hand warm and solid as it gripped her forearm. "I want to know, to be sure, that if something goes wrong, you have the best protection possible. That's Colt, and you know it."

"He's not that great." But he was. He was tough, determined, and almost as strong as her Alpha. She should have seen this assignment coming.

"You are going to be far away from your pack, child," her Alpha said, reminding her of the speech he gave when she left for college. He'd let her go alone then, though he'd sent guards to check on her. This time, she wouldn't be so lucky it seemed. "We won't be able to get you help if something happens. You take Colt, or you don't go."

Definitely not as lucky as when she went to school. Michaela knew when she'd been beaten, which meant she'd have to follow his rules because she wasn't missing this opportunity. While she respected her pack, trusted them with her life, the love and loyalty she felt for her Omega sister was even greater. They'd gone through medical school together, had leaned on one another in the human environment of the hospital during their residencies, had pulled each other through the hard nights of studying, and had together handled the stress of trying not to be found out for what they really were. They'd become true family. She'd do anything for her Omega sister. Including deal with the beast known as Colt.

"Fine." The word felt foul as it passed her lips, but there was nothing she could do. Her Alpha had bested her, had refused to give her a single concession. She'd lost the battle, but she'd win the war. She was leaving.

Keeping her head high even as she seethed with the fact that she'd partially failed, she spun on her heel and headed for the door. "Tell Colt to be ready at dawn. I want to be on the road first thing in the morning."

— —

The trip north should have taken less than a day had the two wolves been allowed to book a plane ticket like a human couple would. But they weren't human, and therefore, they didn't travel like them. Michaela's Alpha had become obsessively concerned about records and paper trails over the years. A fact she understood even though it made her life more difficult. In the digital age they found themselves in, it was getting harder and harder to hide beneath the radar of human attention. So she and Colt bought train tickets under assumed names, making for a much longer trip. And one infinitely more frustrating.

The pair traveled as a married couple, their paperwork showing they were Mr. and Mrs. Chris and Natalie Hoffman— average, human names that made them forgettable. It was hard for Michaela to get into that married woman role she had to play, though. Colt made her nervous, and there was no way she could hide that. She tended to jump when Colt touched her arm, moved away when he shifted closer. He was too big, too dark, too intensely masculine. He overwhelmed her in ways she simply couldn't handle.

That didn't mean Colt was anything other than appropriate, though. Even when they shared a room, Colt slept on the floor, giving her a modicum of privacy and as much space as he could. Never pushing her in any way. Still, Michaela felt uneasy with him around. Felt uncomfortable, as if he was watching her too closely. As if he was monitoring her, waiting for her to mess up. She looked forward to the moment when they could get to their destination, when she could find some breathing room from the shifter.

As she lay in bed on the third and final night of their trip, ignoring the soft snore of her roommate coming from the couch across the room, she thought back over the memories of her friend Ariel, of their past together. Of how the woman had disappeared for a while, and how much Michaela had missed her. There was much catching up to do. One more day. Just one more day and they'd be reunited after far too long apart.

The non-couple couple arrived at their destination bedraggled, exhausted, and downright sick of each other.

"We need a car." Michaela looked around the train station hoping to find a sign for rentals. Nearly breathless as she took in the formidable mountain range in the distance. "Maybe we can rent a 4x4 or something."

Colt apparently had other ideas. "We shift and run."

He walked off, heading toward the tree line at the far end of the parking lot. As if her opinion didn't matter. As if he got to set the rules, the overbearing jackass.

"Hang on." She rushed after him, dragging her suitcase behind her. "We have too much stuff."

He stopped in his tracks, turning in a slow arc to face her. She realized her mistake the second his eyebrows went up.

He glanced at her heavy suitcase, the one with her medical bag sitting on top of it, along with her purse wrapped around the handle. And then he adjusted the backpack he carried. His only bag.

"I told you to pack light."

Michaela glared. "And I told you I needed my medical supplies."

He smirked, his eyes skating past her medical bag to the large suitcase filled with clothes and shoes and…things a woman needed. "Then you leave your other bag, and we run."

"Not happening." Michaela turned and headed for the station, hoping to find some sort of car rental place or car service to take them to the remote location she'd been given. Colt didn't follow her at first, but she knew he would. Their Alpha would have given him clear orders not to leave her alone. So she walked, confident in her plan.

When he did catch up, stalking behind her and basically chasing her into the station, he did so with a growl. She wasn't scared, though.

"Maybe we can get an Uber." She pulled out her cell phone and tapped the app to see what was available.

Colt huffed. "No Uber would take us that far. We should just run."

"I'm not running, I'm not leaving behind my bag, and I'm not letting you dictate how this trip will go."

Colt glared down at her, creeping closer. Looking ready to kill. "Get outside and shift."

Michaela smiled, truly grinned at the challenge thrown in her face. Then she turned on her heel and flounced all the way to the front desk.

"Excuse me," she said to the gentleman behind the glass, giving him her best smile. "Is there a place around here to rent a car? My husband and I need to get to the west side of Shepherd's Ridge." She kicked her smile up a notch, giving him a flirty head cock for good measure. "We're visiting family."

The man stared, looking a little charmed by her. Jackpot. "There's a rental place three blocks into town," he said. "Or if you can wait about twenty minutes, I'm heading up that way. I'd be happy to drop you off with your friends."

Michaela grinned and leaned on her heavy bag, shooting a wink at her traveling companion. "Oh, honey. Isn't that great? He'll take us right to where we need to go."

She'd probably pay for that later, but the glare on his face and the irritation in his eyes were well worth anything he might feel like dishing out.

— —

Reggie, the kind, old ticket seller from the station, was a chatty little man—a widower, apparently. As he drove Michaela and Colt up through the hills, he talked endlessly about his late wife, his kids who lived far away, and the grandkids he rarely got to see. Michaela felt sorry for him. Colt, on the other hand, looked ready to cut the human's throat.

"We there yet?" Colt asked, hanging on to the handle above his window as Reggie made a harsh turn.

"Just about," Reggie said. "Who'd you say you were coming to visit, anyway?"

Michaela smiled again, directing every bit of charm she had into a single look. "Oh, just one of my cousins. She moved up here with her new husband. I haven't seen her in forever."

A bit of truth buried in her lie. A fact she regretted and planned to rectify on this visit.

Reggie scratched at his whiskered chin. "I hadn't realized a young couple had moved out this way."

"They keep to themselves."

Reggie seemed to take that statement at face value. He

kept heading deeper into the forest, following the snaky road that turned back and arched over hills as though he drove it every day. He probably did, which was why, when they reached the top of the hill where Michaela knew they needed to be, she directed him a little farther down the road.

"They said it would be just past one of these switchbacks." She glanced at Colt, and he nodded, letting her know her plan not to show Reggie where the shifters lived was a good one. She waited for a solid mile before pointing at the side of the road.

"There." She smiled at Reggie again. "They told me to stop at the purple mailbox."

Reggie frowned. "I don't know how comfortable I am leaving you two young ones out here by yourselves. Are you sure there isn't someone I can call for you?"

Ha. If only he knew that they were probably the most dangerous creatures in the woods.

Michaela was already clambering out of the car, impatient to see her friend. "Oh, no, we'll be fine. I'm sure they're not far from here. Besides, we can call them ourselves and tell them to come down and meet us along the way. I'm sure that won't be a problem."

Colt joined her beside the car, his backpack thrown over his shoulder. He grabbed her suitcase from her hand, looking like the polite new husband he was supposed to be. "Thanks for everything, Reggie."

The old man waved as he pulled away, driving slowly around the next curve. Colt and Michaela waited until he disappeared before turning back the way they'd come.

"It was a good plan to make him go farther."

Michaela stared at Colt. Gaped, really. Unable to believe he'd complimented her. "Thanks."

"Let's get moving. I want to reach the cabin before dark."

Michaela followed him through the woods and up the

trail. With every step, she cursed herself for wearing the impractical shoes she had, but she'd wanted to look nice. Rookie mistake on her part. The road was long, the trek difficult, and Colt certainly didn't make it any easier. He refused to slow down, pushing her to hurry, ignoring every complaint and request to slow down. The bastard.

"Oh, thank God," she said, pointing at the dark, metal roof peeking through the tree line. "There it is."

Colt grunted, following where she indicated to see the little cabin set back in the far copse of trees. "Quaint."

"Please be nice," Michaela said, ready to beg if necessary. "This woman is very important to me. She's more than my friend. Practically a sister. She's an Omega like I am, and she needs my help. Don't make this harder on either one of us."

Colt stared down at her, his face serious. "I promise, though you're the priority. Not her."

Michaela took him at his word, understanding his opinion. Her Alpha had set the rules, and Colt would follow them to a T. She really had no other choice but to give him leeway to focus on her. Or maybe she was just too tired to fight anymore.

The two followed the trail all the way to the clearing that served as the front yard of the little cabin. Colt had been right about one thing—it was quaint. That word was the only way to describe it. Warm, golden light shone through the windows, flowers bloomed along the steps leading up to the porch, a brightly painted swing hung on one side with matching blankets tossed across the seat as if waiting for the next person to come sit down. The cabin was low, small, and postcard pretty. The perfect place for Ariel.

"I think I like it here," Michaela said, her voice a little too quiet. A little too covetous. She looked around once more, taking in every detail. "It's perfect."

She took a deep breath, relishing the energy in the air.

Anticipation tingled along her body in response to that energy. Something she sensed, something she could almost feel on the wind. This was where she was meant to be. Standing in this forest, right in front of this cabin.

She grinned up at Colt, grabbing his arm, ready to tug him inside. "Come on. I can't wait another minute."

But as they took their first step toward the porch, as the front door swung inward and the woman Michaela had been called to see appeared behind the screen, the energy turned. Twisted darker and more volatile. Danger flitted across Michaela's skin in a warning of sorts, one Colt's low growl told her he felt as well.

Before Ariel could even step outside to welcome them, Colt was in motion.

"Colt, no." Michaela reached for his arm, but it was too late. He'd shifted and was racing toward the corner of the house. Toward the huge wolf barreling down on them. Toward the threat headed her way.

Three

Phego stalked through the woods, trampling through the brush and flushing out game. Without prey animals to attract them, there would be no predators lurking through his woods. And though he could have easily bested a mountain lion in his wolf form, a bear would have taken too much of his attention away from his mission. He wanted Ariel safe and protected, wanted her to be at ease during these last days of her pregnancy. He owed that much to Thaus. There was no greater pressure than the one Thaus had put on him. Responsible for the Dire's family, his mate, his child... Phego could not fail.

As he ran through trees and raced over the hills, circling the little cabin in the woods that had become his home base, his mind wandered. Family and threats went together in his reality. It hadn't always been that way, though. He'd grown up in a pack much like the other wolves in the world. One Alpha leading a large group of shifters who lived, hunted, mated, and fought together. But that all changed the day his brother came to retrieve him from a hunting run. He'd never forget it. How could he? It wasn't every day your own brother led you to your death. Wasn't every day your family turned on you in such a horrific way. But he'd been lucky that a certain Dire Wolf shifter caught sight of what was happening and risked his own life for Phego's. A certain Dire whose mate he now protected.

That was why Phego would try so hard for Thaus. That was why he refused to think of failing for even a second. Thaus, with Luc's help, had saved his life, had rescued him from the death his own parents had planned and his brother had attempted to enact. Phego could not let his real brothers down.

He circled closer to the cabin, not wanting to be out of earshot of Ariel just in case. She knew to yell if she needed him or if anything, even the smallest of feelings, made her nervous. Still, he stayed nearby as he flushed out the small animals who'd been brave enough to live so close to a wolf. As he did so, as his feet pounded on the ground and his heart pulsed in his chest, the memories of his youth kept him in a weird sort of company. He could never relax from his vigilance. His world had shattered once, and though his Dire Wolf brothers had replaced his traitorous family, he still worried. Not about his brothers so much, not anymore, but their mates. The sudden rush of new women in their lives. All seven Dires had gone thousands of years without finding those fated connections—until one mission, one trip to the swamp, changed everything. Within a couple of years of the first mating in their pack's history, four of the seven had found their matches. Stunning odds, really. Unbelievable ones. Not normal ones. He continually questioned why, after so many centuries alone, they suddenly began to fall prey to the manipulations of fate.

The thought that he might find a mate, that he might

match to a shewolf of his own, was enough to set his fur on end and bring out his snarl. He'd never be able to trust her. He would never know if their mated bond was strong enough to hold them together or just tenuous enough to keep him in the path of danger until it was too late to escape.

As Phego turned around the north end of the property, he heard the rumbling sound of an engine drawing near. There were very few cars that came out this way: a couple of old human mountaineers still trying to make it in the harsh peaks rising above his land, a handful of people choosing to live deep in the forests to stay off the grid, even an old miner or two still hoping to hit a vein of gold. The truck sounded familiar, the engine pattern something he'd heard often. He knew that vehicle, knew the man who drove it. What he didn't know was why the truck was stopping so close to his property.

He stood solid and still, ears up and listening, every sense on high alert. Doors slammed, and the murmur of voices that shouldn't have been there added to the sense that something was off. Sounds of new people, of trespassers, whispered along the wind, not loud enough for him to truly know what was going on, just enough to keep him wary. To pull out every protective instinct he had.

After a few moments, the engine rumbled again, the truck moving on along the road. But Phego didn't trust that the threat was gone. Why had the doors slammed? Who had been speaking? And where were they now?

He crept back toward the cabin, running along a path that would lead him toward the road just to be on the safe side. There was no way he could leave Ariel unprotected enough to explore the scene, but he could edge that way. Hunt for more signs. Look for anything out of the ordinary. But as he made his way on a broad arch, the woods remained silent, almost too silent.

Phego picked up his pace, the tension in the air feeding

into his own fears. Something was coming. Something big. Something bad. Something he'd need to protect Ariel from. If he could just find it…

At the murmur of voices, voices he didn't know, he sped to an all-out run. Someone was in the woods. More than one someone. And they were getting closer to the cabin, closer to Ariel.

They were also getting closer to their own deaths.

Phego crossed into the clearing surrounding the cabin just as he heard the front door swing open from the other side of the house. Even so far away, Ariel's scent—fear and bravery and the uniqueness that was her, all mixed together—blasted him, warned him that she was in harm's way. That she was coming outside to investigate the threat. That she was scared of something. He couldn't leave her to face a fear alone. He had to protect her from whatever was coming. Whatever it was that was heading her way.

As he came around the corner of the porch, he zeroed in on the biggest threat. A man, huge and dark and menacing even in his human form, stood ten feet from the porch, looking focused and attentive. Too attentive. Phego would fix that. He clawed at the ground a little harder, growled a little louder, letting the bastard know he wasn't alone. The man spotted him, his lip curling in a threatening move, his shifter scent hitting Phego hard. It would be a tough fight, but Phego would win. He had to. His Dire brother needed him to.

The man took one look at Phego, took one second to curl that lip and growl, and then shifted. Shredded clothing flew out from around his lupine form, and a vicious snarl left his lips before his paws hit the earth.

But Phego was ready for him.

He raced across the clearing, adjusting his path so as to stay between the enemy wolf and the porch. Blocking the target of the attack. Keeping Ariel safe. He met the beast in a crash that sent them both rolling, his teeth bared, his claws out and slicing through flesh from the start. Ready to fight. Ready to kill.

The sound of women screaming burned his ears, the fear from both eating at his concentration. Women... Plural. Fuck, the bastard wasn't alone. He couldn't take his eyes off his threat, though. Couldn't risk a moment of distraction as he slashed and bit. He kept his tail pointed toward the house, kept his prey in front of him, kept his body blocking access to Ariel. The male would not sneak past him. Would not win. He'd deal with the other female once he had the wolf on the ground.

But just as the two clashed again in a brutal dance of death, a scent unlike any other captured his attention. It called to him, stole every ounce of his focus. Overtook his thoughts. He was unable to resist the lure. The turn of his head was automatic, the way his eyes sought the source of that smell an instinct. Something unstoppable and irrefutable.

A woman stood at the edge of the porch, close enough to the steps to be a threat to Ariel, though Phego didn't think she was. Something about her, something about the way she watched the fight, the way she seemed so nervous and afraid, spoke to him. Not a threat. At least, not to Ariel.

But she was the most dangerous thing he'd ever seen.

A distraction in a fight was a deadly thing, especially one as enticing as her. Before he could pull himself from his obsession, before he could turn back to refocus on his enemy, the slice of claws along his shoulder threw him off-balance.

He'd been hit.

The slice sent him stumbling back a few steps, caused him to limp with his injured leg. For one brief moment, he was ready to dive back in and kill the fucker who'd clawed him. But then Ariel appeared, shoving herself between the two wolves, her baby belly out and unprotected.

He'd never known such a feeling of failure. He'd screwed up and caused Ariel to be in more danger, something he'd vowed not to do. But he was still alive. Still ready to go again. Still snarling. Down, but not out. At least until the other woman joined Ariel, putting herself in front of Phego's competitor. Shoving him backward while yelling.

"Colt, stop. He's not a threat to me." She shoved again, the two moving farther away. Their distance helped to soothe Phego's rage, helped to give him the clarity to calm himself. As did Ariel whispering in his ear.

"It's okay. She's my friend, and he's here to guard her. He scared me at first, but they won't hurt me. I'm fine now. Calm down, I need you to shift so I can look at the damage to your shoulder."

Phego wouldn't shift back, though. Couldn't risk going human in such a dangerous situation. Just because Ariel trusted her so-called friend didn't mean he would. And the male—Colt. Guard or not, he wasn't welcome on Phego's land. Thaus would have thrown that Colt's ass back to the road for daring to be near his mate, and he'd want Phego to do the same.

Ariel rubbed her hand down Phego's shoulder, soothing him, calling to his human side as she inspected his injury. "C'mon, Phego. Come back to me. There's no danger here, but there is an injury. I need to look at it. Will you shift for me?"

He growled low in his throat, keeping his eyes on the two interlopers.

Ariel sighed. "Quit being stubborn."

But he refused to shift, refused even to sit down so she could get a better angle while looking over his shoulder. He needed to keep her safe, and he was a better fighter in his wolf form. Though, he'd need to figure out what the fuck that scent was and why it had distracted him so. He hadn't messed up that bad in a fight since he was a kid, and the fact that it happened at such a vital time only fueled his rage.

Ariel ignored his snarling and raised hackles, though. She ran her fingers along his injured shoulder, spreading his fur so she could get a better look. Phego wasn't willing to flinch, wasn't about to let that bastard across the clearing see an ounce of pain on his muzzle, but it hurt. It hurt a lot. The cuts ran deep, all the way to the bone, he guessed. But he'd been hurt worse and by better than the other male. Fucker never would have gotten close to him had he not been distracted. Which reminded him, where was the woman?

As Ariel finished with his shoulder, he searched every bit of the property that he could see. The male wolf guarded the tree line, looking right at Phego. Ready to fight again, his head down, his hackles raised, his body language all challenge. Phego snarled and took a step toward him, refusing to give the bastard a single shot.

"I want you to quit that." Ariel stood, stepping forward in a move that only exemplified her bravery. Moving closer to the enemy she didn't know. She wasn't comfortable around strangers, especially not strange men. Her taking a step in his direction was a solid sign of trust. "Neither of you is a threat to the other or to us. Michaela, where are you?"

The other male growled low and hard, taking a step toward Ariel. She shuffled back, instincts taking over, fear ratcheting up a notch. Phego refused to allow that. He stalked forward, brushing her body with his bigger one, keeping his eyes locked on the threat. Ariel patted his head like a dog and sighed, though her body also seemed to relax with his touch.

"Seriously. He's not a threat to me. Right, Michaela?" Her voice rose on the name, grew louder. Phego wasn't sure why she was calling for the female when the male, the true danger to her, was right in front of them. At least, not until a woman walked out from the trees.

Her black hair sat in tiny ringlets, creating a soft, cloud-like halo all around her head. Her dark skin glowed in the bright light of the early afternoon, luminous in a way he'd never seen on another woman. Tall and slender with a high neck made for biting and licking, she captivated him. Yet she wasn't looking at him, a fact that he wanted remedied immediately. He wanted her eyes on him. Wanted her hands in his fur or on his skin. He wanted.

His entire body locked down, every sense alerted to her. Nothing else could break through, nothing could penetrate. All he saw, all he felt, all he focused on was her.

Which sent a sliver of ice careening down his spine.

She was a threat to him. He didn't know how and he didn't know why, but she could destroy him.

The other male wolf walked beside her as she approached, staying a single step in front of her, leading her and offering a wall of wolf to block any attack. A good move, but one Phego could have taken advantage of if he'd wanted to.

The woman scratched her wolf's head, an act that seemed unnatural and forced. "Please stop. And will you shift back? We don't need another incident here."

Colt glanced up at her then back at the Phego, obviously still wary. But eventually, he shifted. He stood on two feet beside the darker female, naked as the day he was born, still looking as if he'd kill for her. Phego didn't care about him, though. Not really. The female seemed the greater threat. So he kept his hip against Ariel's legs as he took a step back, forcing her away, creating distance between them all.

But he couldn't resist the pull to the other woman. He couldn't ignore her even as she refused to meet his gaze. He wanted her eyes on him, wanted to know what they looked like dead on. Wanted to feel her looking at him. Something he couldn't understand.

"Phego," Ariel said. "This is Michaela. She's my friend, my Omega sister, and my midwife. Michaela, this is Phego. He'll be playing the role of bodyguard while my mate is away."

The woman, Michaela, smiled, nearly bouncing on her toes in excitement. "God, I've missed you. And this is Colt. He'll be playing the role of a pain in the ass while I'm here. Now, no one go all badass protector on us. I need to hug my friend."

Without a word from Ariel, the two women came together, arms wrapping around one another, soft giggles and whispers shared as they reconnected. The affection between the two, the connection, burned obvious and pure. Something that caused him to stop growling and simply watch. Phego hadn't experienced a hug in a long time. Some of the Dire mates were huggers, some of the females more affectionate than others, but they all tended to stay away from him. Perhaps that was his fault, perhaps theirs. Whatever the reason, he coveted the easy camaraderie the women shared. That hug was so strong, that connection so clear…he didn't think he'd ever experienced anything like it.

As the two women came apart, Michaela finally looked his way. It was in that moment when their eyes met that their souls connected. That the bonds between them grew and infiltrated every inch of his being. Fate wrapped itself through his head, the connection solidifying into something overwhelming and nearly painful.

Mate.

The word echoed through his mind, pulling him deeper into the abyss of his memories while simultaneously thrusting him straight into a future he didn't want. Shit.

This wasn't supposed to happen to him. Not then, not ever. This wasn't part of his plan.

Michaela took a single step back, her eyes wide, her mouth falling open as she stared. He knew she felt the connection, which meant she had power over him. Something he needed to rebel against. Something he could not allow to affect Ariel.

He ripped his gaze from Michaela's, circling in front of Ariel and herding her back, forcing her up the stairs and onto the porch.

"Apparently, we're going inside," Ariel said, glaring down at Phego. But he didn't care. He needed her safe, needed her calm and unafraid, which meant he needed her inside.

Ariel opened the door to go into the cabin with Phego following close behind. A moment later, Michaela and her male, Colt, followed. Phego pushed and growled and demanded until Ariel fell into the corner seat, the most protected position in the place. And then he sat directly in front of her, his fur brushing her legs. His mind and heart shielded from the lure of his mate.

"Well," Ariel said. "Isn't this awkward."

But Phego didn't feel awkward. He felt threatened. In danger.

He felt as if his life was over all because of the woman across the room.

*M*ichaela had never been so twitchy, so perfectly in tune with the energy around her. The wolf ignited something within her, every look from him setting her soul on fire. The tug of connection tied them together, binding and strong, the pull of something bigger than both of them demanding her attention.

Holy shit, she'd found her mate.

She hadn't really searched for one, hadn't been out looking or attending The Gathering events to try to find that connection. Hell, she hadn't even taken a pleasure mate to her bed in years. She'd simply gone about her life. She went to college, she went to med school, she became a doctor. During that time, of course, she had the pleasure of a man's company now and again. No boyfriends, as the humans called them. Nothing serious. To Michaela, arousal was much like any other irritation; arousal was the itch, and sex was the scratch. Nothing more, nothing less.

But with one look, things had changed. With one gaze

into those pale, silver eyes, she'd become something else. Something more. She was his, whether she liked the idea or not. And while the concept of mates was something that intrigued her, the wolf the fates had picked for her wasn't exactly who she would have chosen for herself. He was so rough, so powerful and intense. Brutal, really. And that was just in his wolf form. He still hadn't shifted human. She had no idea what he looked like in that form. She wanted to, though. Would have given almost anything to lay her eyes on his skin and see what all that muscle looked like without the fur covering it.

But along with rough and hard and mean, he was also apparently stubborn. He settled in front of Ariel in wolf form. Not budging, not laying off the wolf glare for a second. Though considering the features of that wolf, she shouldn't have been surprised.

Coming from an old-school pack, Michaela knew the signs of a Dire Wolf. She'd grown up with the legends and stories, the tales of the large breed that served as the soldiers of the shifter world. She also knew they were supposed to be extinct.

Her mate's heavy body, his thick neck, the sheer size of him indicated he was something else. Something more than just your average, everyday shifter. But it was the spots along his back, on his shoulders and upper head, that locked in that Dire lineage in her mind. If anyone else noticed, they didn't say anything. Neither did she. But she wondered where he'd come from, how he'd ended up in the woods of Montana with her friend, and how he'd survived centuries living among other shifters without being found out. She wondered a lot.

"How are you feeling?" Michaela asked, her eyes flitting to Ariel. A hard thing to do considering how magnetic her mate seemed to be. But she refused to give in, refused to stop and stare. She was there for one reason.

The shewolf smiled, also ignoring the wolves growling subtly around them. Her hand rested on her belly in a symbol of protection as old as time. "Good. Really good. I just can't wait to meet this little guy."

"So you know it's a boy?" Michaela glanced at the wolf on the floor, tearing her eyes from Ariel's for a moment before fighting to regain focus. Unable not to at least peek. Unable to completely look away. If she didn't pull it together, everyone was going to figure out what had happened. That she'd found her fated mate. And that he could barely look at her without sending a violent growl her way.

Lovely.

Ariel shrugged, still rubbing her belly. "No, not really. But Thaus thinks so. He's kind of convinced of it."

"And if the baby's a girl?" Michaela hated to ask, but some of the males of her species were a little…out of touch. Male offspring implied strength and potency while a female was more of a burden at times. Unless they were an Omega; then the tables tended to be turned. Omegas were rare, though. Very rare.

But Ariel only smiled and shook her head, completely at ease. "If it's a girl, he's never going to let her out of his sight. He's very protective."

The wolf at Ariel's feet huffed, as if agreeing with her. Michaela couldn't help sweeping his body with her eyes once more, following the ridged curve of his back to the thick muscles of his thighs. Just the thought, the idea of what all that would look like in human form, had her clenching her thighs together. She wanted him to shift.

Michaela coughed and forced herself to focus back in on Ariel, trying her hardest to keep her eyes on her patient and not the male at her feet. "Well, as a friend, I'm so happy for you. You look beautiful, healthy, and unbelievably at peace. But as a midwife, I know looks can be deceiving."

Michaela smiled and stood. "How about we check a few things out?"

But as she took a step toward Ariel, the wolf at her feet rose. He stood between the two women, his hackles raised, a silent snarl curling his lips. Michaela refused to be cowed. She was here for a reason, and that reason was making sure that her friend and the baby made it through the delivery safe and healthy.

But Ariel's eyes widened and focused on something over Michaela's shoulder. Colt. He'd moved closer, set himself into a defensive position at her side. And he'd scared the pregnant shewolf, if the way she stared at him was any indication. Odd. Ariel had never been skittish when they were in school.

Wanting to calm the situation, Michaela held a hand out toward Colt. There would be no fighting, no more wrestling or battling. No intimidating her friend and patient. She'd had enough of the dick-swinging contest.

Colt took a step back, giving her room to do her thing, but not Phego. The wolf refused to budge, refused to quiet his growl, refused to give her a chance. Stubborn, that one.

Michaela cocked her hip, raising an eyebrow and glaring down at her new mate. "I'm here in a professional capacity. She's my patient, and I would never do anything to hurt her. Why don't you quit growling at me and get out of my way?"

The wolf's eyes widened, a comical look of shock on his canine face. Maybe nobody talked to him that way on a normal basis. Boy, was he going to have to learn.

Ariel sighed, rolling her eyes. "Phego, let her through."

But the wolf didn't move, didn't give up a single step. He just stared Michaela down. Good thing she'd gotten used to those long, hard Alpha stares.

"Look, Phego. You don't mind if I call you by your name, do you? Good. Now look, we'll stay right here so you can watch the exam. It'll all be G-rated. Ariel and I don't need to get up close and personal quite yet." As Michaela moved forward again, Colt shadowed her. Ariel sat deeper into the chair, her eyes flitting to him, her body stiffening up. Shit, this wouldn't work. Phego snarled at Colt, rising slightly as if preparing to fight, looking as if he was ready to defend Ariel to the death. Michaela had no doubt he would. Irritated with both men in the room, she held up her hand, ordering Colt to stop.

"I'm fine," Michaela said, directing her words at Colt. "He won't hurt me, and I won't hurt her. This is nothing more than me getting handsy with the baby bump. But I need you to back up, Colt. You're making my patient uncomfortable."

"I'm okay, Phego," Ariel whispered, her words barely reaching Michaela's ears. After several long seconds of intense masculine glaring, and a few nudges from the leg of the pregnant woman in the room, the two males stepped out of the way. Even so, they stayed awfully close. Uncomfortably so.

"Good thing I learned how to play Twister." Michaela stretched over the Dire Wolf, reaching for Ariel as best she could. Before she made contact, she paused, holding up her hands, meeting her friend's eyes to get permission. Ariel nodded, still smiling through whatever emotions were pulling at her. Glowing, practically. Michaela couldn't hold back her own smile.

"Let's see what we've got here." Michaela placed her hands on Ariel's belly, closing her eyes and focusing on the life within. The power of the Omega warmed her, swirling around in a way that other wolves would never know. Most of the time, Michaela used her human training: stats and figures, labels and signs. But when it came to babies, shifter babies especially, she had something most people did not. She had an innate power within her. A gift to sense and feel and know with just a touch. And that gift calmed her worries in a matter of seconds.

"Well, I can't tell you if it's a boy or a girl, but the heart rate is strong, your blood pressure is fine, and everything feels right." She looked up at Ariel. "The baby is coming soon."

Arial's smile faded a little, and she grabbed for Michaela's hand. "Not too soon. Thaus is…away."

Michaela cocked her head, sensing something more Ariel wanted to say. Knowing that she wouldn't, whether that was because of the guard at her side, because of the stranger standing behind Michaela, or for some other reason she might never know.

Michaela's lips turned up in a supportive smile, one she'd practiced a million times to soothe her patients. "I'm sure he'll make it back. Everything will be fine."

But as she glanced at her new mate, as she met Phego's unusual silver eyes, she sensed his understanding. His stress. Her words weren't necessarily true. That baby was going to come—and soon—whether the daddy was back or not.

— —

Hours later, after a healthy dinner, a few cups of tea, and a lot of conversation, the foursome sat in Ariel's living room. Calm and quiet, finally. Though an edge of wariness still vibrated around the males—one in human form and dressed, the other still wearing his fur—the women were doing just fine. Typical.

Feet up, eyes droopy, Michaela sighed. "It's getting late."

Ariel yawned and nodded. "Yeah, it might be time to hit the hay."

"The hay? So I'm sleeping in a barn, am I? Wouldn't be the first time."

With a laugh, Ariel stood, wobbly on her feet. Michaela jumped up to help her, but her coordination felt off. Sluggish. She moved a bit slower than Colt, who reached the pregnant Omega first. Ariel jerked her arm away from him, though, tripping herself and falling into the side of the chair. Michaela was there to catch her in an instant, evaluating every move, every reaction from her friend. Something had gone wrong somewhere. Something had hurt her.

Michaela's mate jumped up from the floor and growled, but Ariel only shushed him. "I'm fine." Ariel took a deep breath when she was on her feet and stable. "It gets harder and harder."

Michaela frowned, unsure if she meant dealing with Colt or being pregnant. She hoped it was the latter. "Just wait until that baby drops. Walking around is going to be quite the adventure."

Ariel rolled her eyes. "Great. Just what I need. More difficulty getting around."

Michaela yawned and stretched, ready for bed. Definitely ready to get Colt away from Ariel so the woman could relax again.

"I'm turning in. We can resume this conversation tomorrow." Michaela gave Ariel a hug, squeezing her tight as she whispered, "I'm so glad you called me to help."

"I'm so glad you were able to come."

"There was no way I wouldn't. Even though I had to bring Colt with me for backup."

The shifter in question rolled his eyes and headed for the stairs. "Thank you for your hospitality, Miss Ariel."

Ariel's eyes widened as they met Michaela's, shock evident on her pretty face. Colt hadn't spoken much all night. And the words he had said had been gruff, direct, and not necessarily polite. That sentence was practically turning over a new leaf.

Ariel recovered first, murmuring a quiet, "You're welcome, Colt."

Michaela turned to grab her bag, but the soft sensation

of fur against her leg made her freeze. Her mate was there. Standing beside her. Almost bumping into her with his shoulder. It was the first time they'd touched; the first time they'd made any sort of contact. And even though the moment was fur on skin, it nearly knocked her to her knees.

Before she could act on that, before she could reach down and run her hand over his fur, before she could do anything other than freeze, the moment was shattered by her brooding, crabby packmate.

"Michaela, are you coming up?" Colt's voice carried from upstairs, the words innocuous enough if one knew their situation fully. Not that Phego or Ariel did. Her mate's eyes narrowed, a growl breaking the silence. Michaela had forgotten about the sleeping arrangements her Alpha had laid down, knew it wouldn't look good heading up to a single bedroom with another man. But what could she say? Colt and Ariel didn't know she'd mated to Phego, didn't have any idea the possessiveness he probably felt toward her. He hadn't shifted human, and Michaela hadn't told her bodyguard. Colt probably assumed the situation was as normal as it had been while they were traveling. That the two of them would act as a couple and sleep in the same room. Such an awkward spot to be in when your newly found mate had no idea it was all a ruse.

As Ariel busied herself in the kitchen, Michaela attempted to whisper to her mate, to explain. To make him understand. "It's not—"

But he only snarled, the sound sending a shiver up her spine.

"Phego?" Ariel called, padding back into the living space. "What's going on?"

The wolf didn't answer, didn't even look at her. He stalked to the front door, standing on his back legs until his paw hit the lever just right. The second the door popped open, the wolf was gone. Running out into the darkness of the night like a wraith hell-bent on wreaking havoc. Or hiding. Michaela wasn't sure which.

"What just happened?" Ariel asked, coming to stand beside Michaela. Both women looked outside, but the night was too dark. The forest made up of deepening shadows and pits of lightlessness. Still, Michaela knew he was out there, watching her, probably angry and upset. He wouldn't have left Ariel alone with two strangers, not after all the fight he'd put up earlier. He was dancing in the dark, alone, watching them. Listening. But there was nothing she could do at that point. Nothing she could say that would relieve him of her judgment without admitting their mated bond. And if he wasn't willing to tell people about that, neither was she.

"I don't know. Though, I don't know a thing about him."

That was the truth. What she didn't say, though— what she didn't add to that sentence—was that she hated her ignorance in regards to Phego. She wanted to learn everything about him, wanted to know his face and his body, his voice and his touch. She wanted to know him, and she would. Eventually.

She hoped.

Five

Phego clawed the wet ground, digging himself a shallow hole just to the side of the porch. Typical. His mate was inside, sharing a room with a man he didn't know, and he was outside in the dirt. Not that he wanted a mate. Not that he cared for one. But the fates had chosen her for him, had brought them together at the worst time, dangling her in front of his face like some sort of cosmic fuck you.

He shouldn't have cared, shouldn't have been attracted to her. He should've trusted his instincts when he'd first seen the couple standing outside the cabin and acted on them. He'd wanted to kill the male and kick the female off his property. That's what he should've done. No second chances, no option for betrayal, cabin locked down and secure for Ariel's safety…and his.

But that's not what he'd done.

The screen door creaked open, and Phego found himself looking. Staring. Hoping it was Michaela, the woman he'd been chosen for. The one he shouldn't want or crave or desire.

And he definitely should not have been disappointed when Ariel stepped outside instead.

Ariel…his mission. His Dire sister. He needed to get his head on straight.

Phego chuffed softly, not wanting to scare her but letting her know he was there. Letting her know she wasn't alone outside.

Ariel sat on the edge of the porch, her feet resting on the step below, her body curling over her rounded belly in a protective posture.

"Are you going to shift?" she asked, keeping her voice soft and calm. Barely disturbing the quiet of the night. "Are you going to talk to me about what happened today?"

Phego snorted, giving her all the answer he could. Ariel sighed and pulled the sweater she wore around her shoulders tighter. She looked cold. The night had a chill to it, the expectation of one final frost hovering around them. The last of the winter winds were blowing down from the mountains, cooling everything off before spring officially hit. As a wolf, Phego didn't notice. But in human form, he could understand why Ariel seemed so uncomfortable. He growled, doing what he could tell her to get back inside where he hoped it was safe. Not that he knew, not that he could be sure. Not with the two interlopers inside.

"Colt makes me nervous, but I'm okay. I'm calming down around him, and hopefully I won't be so jumpy once I'm used to his presence in my house." Ariel tapped her feet, staring out into the darkness, ignoring Phego's signal. "She's your mate, isn't she?"

Phego went silent and still, unwilling to admit anything. Not wanting to have Ariel think that fact changed anything. It didn't. Couldn't. The fates may have chosen her, but he hadn't.

Ariel turned, leaning against the railing, her eyes focusing on him. Even in the dark he could feel her gaze, could sense her watching. Investigating. He wanted to escape that stare but was too afraid to move. Too worried about her to leave her in the dark. He was trapped.

"You can trust her, you know," Ariel whispered. Lying to him the way everyone else would as well. A mate was something special, they'd say. Something to cherish. They'd be wrong. They'd all be wrong, and he'd be the one to pay for their mistakes. A mate was nothing more than an enemy you made the mistake of letting inside your walls so they could destroy you. One the fates threw into your path at random. No. He couldn't trust Michaela.

Phego released a small snarl, just enough to let Ariel know how he felt about those words. About trusting anyone outside of his very small circle.

"She's my friend," Ariel said, her voice soft but firm, demanding in a way. "I love her like a sister, and I trust her with my life. With the baby's life. Thaus trusted her, and he never met her. That's why I'm learning to be okay with Colt—Michaela wouldn't have brought him here if he was a threat to me. I know you have issues—"

Phego jumped to his feet and slunk away, disappearing into the darkness, unwilling to listen to the woman speak about his past. The past she shouldn't have known about. He had *issues*? If she knew the whole truth, she'd know he had more than issues. He had a full subscription...or ten. But those memories and residual fears kept him safe. Kept him alive. Kept him from making the same mistakes again and again. What he'd been through, what he'd managed to survive, was not something you just got over. He had good reason not to trust the shewolf inside. Damn good reason.

Phego stayed outside the cabin for hours after everyone

went to sleep. He'd rest until the itch to leave grew too strong then work a trail, running through the woods to get away from Michaela. Unable to sit still, but also unable to leave *her*. Not the her he was supposed to be worried about—the other one.

There was no noise from the couple upstairs, not that he was listening. Still, the idea of Michaela in a bed she shared with Colt infuriated him. Made his heart burn in ways it never had before, made him tense and angry, wanting to lash out. Wanting to draw blood.

But as Phego turned the corner on his 274th trip around the cabin, a different sort of feeling caught his attention. The feeling of being watched. Of someone else in the woods... someone who shouldn't be there. Phego came to a quick stop and glanced around, investigating. Seeking the source of the uncomfortable sensation. The cabin was dark, the woods as well. He could sense the three people inside. Hear their breathing. The watcher was not there, wasn't close to the cabin at all. He was in the woods. In the trees. In the deeper darkness of the wilderness.

Phego paced in small circles, keeping his eyes open, his ears pricked. Something, something, something; it was out there. He could feel it, sense it, practically taste it on the air. Danger lurked in the woods, and this time, it carried more of a threat than the earlier visitors had. Funny how the watcher and the guests of Ariel's showed up on the same day. Funny, and almost expected.

He'd known not to trust them.

He was just about to stop circling, to begin walking around the cabin once more in a tighter arc, when the sound of a twig cracking from behind him sounded like the shot from a gun. He took off like a rocket, running through the woods as fast as he could, his paws barely touching the ground. Running, chasing, hunting his prey. But whatever was in the woods, whatever the animal was that had been watching him, seemed almost invisible. It had disappeared into the darkness like a shadow melting into the night. Phego couldn't even pick up a scent trail.

But scent or not, sight or not, Phego made out the occasional rustle of leaves being disturbed and the sharp snick of broken sticks and branches. The thing was still there, still running, still close enough to hunt but moving swiftly toward the hills beyond Phego's property. Phego kept after it, slowing his pace so he could listen better, keeping his ears up and forward.

Before he ran even a hundred yards, though, Phego slid to a stop. *Ariel.* The thing in the woods could have been a trick, a way to get him away from their true target. He could have been playing right into an enemy's hands by chasing nothing more than a sensation and a few rustles through the woods. A rookie mistake. He couldn't be that dumb.

Without a second thought, Phego ran back to the cabin, his steps quick and his growl constant. He focused his senses on Ariel, on making sure she was safe. On feeling every bit of energy from her.

Reaching the little building didn't even slow him down. He raced up the porch and through the front door, thankful Ariel had left it cracked for him. Once inside, he finally slowed, his claws clacking on the wood floors with every loped step. Not that he cared. He had more important things to worry about—a Dire sister and a baby. The family he'd chosen as part of his own. The ones he had vowed to protect.

Letting his senses take over, Phego investigated the house. Nothing out of the ordinary, nothing unexpected. Four heartbeats, three people breathing the cool mountain air, all exactly where they were supposed to be. Mostly. Upstairs, he sensed space between the two bodies. Heard their hearts beating from farther apart than he would have expected if they'd been sharing a bed. Perhaps he'd been mistaken. Perhaps his mate—

No. Ariel. The baby. His mission. He had to stay focused, had to stay on guard. Had to forget the trick the fates had thrown at him.

Brushing aside his desire to pad upstairs and see for himself what was going on, Phego crept back to Ariel's room, silent and tense. Ready to fight. Ready to kill if need be. But up on the high bed, buried under a sea of quilts, Ariel slept soundly. She lay curled on her side with one arm over her belly and her legs pulled up. She was cold, it seemed. Phego bit down on the corner of the extra quilt at the end of the bed and dragged it forward, covering her with the last blanket on the bed, just in case.

This was where his focus needed to be. Where his thoughts needed to stay. He couldn't fail Thaus, couldn't let anything happen to her. Finding his mate was a distraction, one he couldn't let get under his skin. He'd been outside earlier because of his mate, had been running through the woods because of her, too. He needed to stay close to Ariel so he could keep her safe and secure. So nothing could come between them and put her at risk.

With a sigh and a burning in his chest he refused to contemplate, Phego circled the rug at the end of the bed before he plopped down. No one would get close to Ariel. Not from outside the cabin, and not from inside, either. Whatever he'd sensed in the woods, whatever he thought he heard, could have been a trick. Could have been a distraction. Could have been a damn deer out on a stroll through the woods, for fuck's sake. It was not his mission, though.

Phego hunkered down close to his ward, nose pointed at the door, tail brushing the leg of the bed. He wouldn't leave her side again—not for his new mate, not for her so-called bodyguard, not for some ridiculous notion of something being in the woods…not for anything.

He would stick to Ariel like glue until Thaus came back, then he'd kick her friends right out of his woods and set his shit back to right.

Six

Michaela's first full day in the little cabin at the edge of the woods dawned bright and warm, the chill of the night burned off the mountain air by the sun above. Her bed was soft, her muscles relaxed, and her mood pleasant. A nice way to wake up for sure. She stretched under the covers, her body languid and her mind clear for one, brief moment.

She'd always been more of a morning person than not, taking advantage of the quiet just after dawn to get a jump-start on her day. She saw each soft, quiet morning as a time to reset herself before the stress of everyday life kicked in, before the reality around her weighed her down and dragged her mood into the darker places. Those precious few minutes were her favorite moments. She relished them, luxuriated in them. But there was no holding back real life.

Especially not when the silence she so loved was broken by the snore of a man she did not.

Michaela glanced over the edge of the bed and saw Colt lying on the rug in his wolf form. Sleeping. He wasn't the man she wanted to see first thing in the morning, though. She wasn't sure if she'd be able to make that clear to her new mate, though. She doubted they would ever be able to get to the intimate point of sharing a bedroom. Not with a man like Phego. He was so closed off, so harsh, so angry it seemed. Hell, he hadn't even shifted human yet, hadn't allowed her the privilege of seeing him in his weaker form. He didn't even trust her enough to shift, and that was a problem. She didn't expect him to wrap his life around hers and simply accept her as his mate, but he could show her a little respect. Maybe even dig down deep for some manners. But that all seemed unlikely if the previous evening was any indication of how the next few weeks would go.

Weeks...with her mate in his wolf form...ignoring her. Wonderful.

Blank slate of the morning destroyed by her thoughts, Michaela stood from the bed and crept out the door. There was nothing she could do right then about Phego, so she set her sights on another target she desired.

Coffee.

She might've been awake, but that didn't mean she didn't need a little jolt. Ariel had to have coffee somewhere in the house. The two had guzzled it during their residency days, surviving on caffeine and beef jerky sticks to get through the long hours at the hospital. The habit had stayed with her, and she was sure Ariel wasn't much different.

She slipped downstairs, careful not to make too much noise. Waking up a sleeping pregnant woman was bad news. No one needed that stress added to their day. Michaela crossed the living room silently, heading straight for the kitchen. But before she could get there, before she could head around the counter that separated it from the open concept living and dining area, the sound of claws on wood floors stopped her in her tracks. She didn't have to turn, didn't have to wonder who was behind her. She could sense him. Feel his dark energy wrapping around her. Practically taste the want her body let boil to the surface at his presence.

"Good morning, Phego," she murmured, keeping her voice quiet so as not to disturb anyone else. She waited for something, some sort of response, though why she thought he'd grace her with anything other than a hard stare, she wasn't sure. She'd assumed he had to respond somehow if only to keep up social norms, but she'd been wrong. He did nothing, moved not an inch, didn't even huff a breath.

Michaela sighed and continued into the kitchen. The coffeepot sat next to the refrigerator, cups on the little stand next to it, but there was no sign of actual coffee. She glanced behind her, meeting the eyes of her mate. He'd come closer, a fact that surprised her. In fact, he was standing in the entryway to the kitchen, watching her. Staring with what looked like interest. A fact that she'd gladly take advantage of.

"Coffee?" Michaela swept her hand toward the cabinets, hoping he'd be able to figure out what she wanted from him at that moment. Coffee was only the smallest desire, really, but it was a start. What she needed, what she truly wanted, was for him to shift, for him to show his human side, for him to talk to her. She wouldn't be getting that anytime soon, though, so coffee seemed like the better option to push for.

Phego padded across the kitchen, coming to stand beside her. His thick fur brushed her bare leg, the top of his shoulder coming up almost to her rib cage. He dwarfed her, took up almost the entire room. He even made the cabin itself somehow feel too small to hold him. How other shifters he'd been around hadn't figured out he was a Dire Wolf was beyond her. There was no doubt in her mind, yet all the legends spoke of the Dires being extinct. Someone was very, very good at blending in as they stood out.

Phego raised his head and leaned forward, bumping his nose into the bottom of a cabinet to the right of the stove before taking a step back. Giving her room once more.

"Thank you," Michaela whispered before heading to

the cabinet. She did indeed find coffee inside, along with basket liners, sweeteners, and powdered creamer. Phego had directed her to the coffee jackpot.

At home, she would have brewed half a pot, but she lived alone. Some pregnant women didn't drink caffeine, so she wasn't sure if Ariel would have any coffee at all, but she knew Colt would and she would. The wolf, well, she had no clue. But maybe. She didn't want to deny him if it was something he liked.

A full pot, it was.

As she waited for the coffee to brew, she collected every scrap of courage she had. She wanted to speak with her mate. Wanted to understand him, get to know him. But he wasn't going to make it easy on her, that she knew up front. So she wouldn't make it easy on him either.

"Hey, Phego," Michaela said, infusing her voice with an upbeat tone she didn't feel. "Does Ariel know you're a Dire Wolf?"

The beast didn't respond, didn't move. She was pretty sure he wasn't even breathing. A sure sign she'd probably hit a nerve.

Michaela shrugged. "It's the spots, really. I remember seeing them in a book at our pack historical center. One of those ones on wolf-shifter legend. The size of you is enough to turn heads, but the spots are undeniable. You're supposed to be extinct."

Nada. Nothing. Not a whine or a growl or a huff. Figured.

As soon as the coffee was done and she'd poured herself a cup, Michaela headed to the seating area on the edge of the island, settling onto a barstool. Her wolf didn't move closer, but he didn't run away either. He didn't leave. She considered that a win. He might not want to answer her, but that didn't mean he didn't want to listen. And she could be a damn fine storyteller when she wanted to be.

"My dad named me Michaela after his brother. My uncle was killed during the European shifter wars of the early 19th century. I assume you know about those, but our pack was hard-hit during that time. Our family was almost decimated before my ancestors managed to escape to the New World. When I was born, an Omega female, the first the pack had ever had, my birth was celebrated. I was brought up loved and cared for, honored by my packmates, and protected by my family. My parents are still alive, and I have three brothers and a sister. I chose to go to medical school when it became apparent that human medicine was advancing quickly, and that I could be of service to the community of wolf shifters and the human towns our land borders. It was a tough go to convince my Alpha to let me leave, but I did it."

Michaela waited, taking a sip of her coffee to give him time to…what, she didn't know. Chuff? Snarl? Walk away? He did none of those things, though. He sat quiet and still, attentive, even. As if he was listening to her rambles, wanting more. Something she could provide him.

"It was during med school that I met Ariel. She was so spunky, so feisty and confident. I liked her from the start, though it was quite the surprise to walk into an auditorium one day and smell another shifter in the room. Things were tense for all of about two minutes before we realized we had advantages over the humans and could help each other out. We studied together, lived together for a while, and kept each other sane during MCATs and residency. She's one of my best friends, practically family to me. The last thing you need to worry about is me doing anything to harm her. I'm here to help, to keep her focused during her delivery, and to make sure she and that baby stay healthy. I know you don't trust me right now, but hopefully you will at the end of this."

Michaela stopped and sipped her coffee again, considering, unsure if the direction of her thoughts was the way to go. But there was more to be said, more he needed to hear, and he was still sitting and watching her. So she took a deep breath and prepared for a reaction.

"Colt is my bodyguard. Even now, even with me being well into adulthood and self-sufficient, my Alpha worries about me. I'm an Omega, and that seems to be a wanted commodity in our society lately. Colt's here to keep me safe, nothing more. He follows me wherever I go, but we're not... He's not—"

Michaela sighed and looked down at the table. Her wolf hadn't even been in human form yet, hadn't spoken to her. How could she say Colt wasn't meaningful to her life when that implied her mate *was* meaningful in some way? She didn't know anything about him, didn't know how he would react. Didn't know if he felt a single bit of attraction for her. That sort of admission, stating you had possible feelings when you had absolutely no idea if the other person had an inkling of attraction or not, was hard. Sort of terrifying.

Sort of...intimate.

"It's hard to have a conversation like this when I don't know what you're thinking," she whispered. "I can't even read your body language or your facial expression. Can you shift, please? Can we—"

Before she could finish her thought, though, Colt came thundering down the stairs, racing into the living room and heading straight for the island where Michaela sat.

"You know better than to leave my side," Colt snapped, a growl rising in his throat. He wore nothing but a pair of boxers, his muscled body fully on display as he grabbed her arm and tugged her off her seat. Not exactly what she needed, considering the conversation she was trying to have with her mate.

Speaking of mate, Phego was on his feet, head down, hackles raised. His growl rumbled through the room, his eyes locked on the other male. With two steps, he pushed his way between Colt and her, shoving the male back until he couldn't hold on to her anymore. Whether he was simply breaking up a random disagreement or defending his mate, Michaela didn't know. She wouldn't know if he wouldn't shift to talk to her. A fact that was seriously hindering her ability to deal with the stress of having an unconfirmed mate and an overzealous bodyguard in the same room.

"I just came for coffee," Michaela said, directing her words to Colt even as her eyes stayed locked on Phego's.

"You should have woken me. I didn't know you'd left the bed."

Michaela winced, unable not to. Left *the bed*. Not the room or the floor, the bed. That wouldn't go well.

"You were still asleep…on the floor," she stressed, hoping Phego understood her intention with that statement. "Besides, I wasn't in any danger."

Ariel padded into the living room from down the hall, her hair wild, her eyes sleepy. "What's this about danger? Oh, is that coffee I smell?"

But Michaela wasn't looking at her, she was watching as Phego stalked out the door. As he left her behind. Ariel also focused on the wolf as he pushed the screen door open, looking worried. Ariel knew Phego better than Michaela did, a fact that only made his exit and her obvious concern that much more upsetting. Could nothing go right between them?

Once Phego was back outside, his heavy breaths loud and clear from his place under the window again, Ariel turned that inquisitive gaze Michaela's way. It only took that one look, that single expression, and Michaela understood. Ariel knew about her and Phego. She knew, and she was going to bring it up once the two women were alone.

Michaela set her coffee cup down and headed back into the kitchen to grab a cup for her friend. Taking a moment to collect herself before coming back out with a distraction in the form of a warm cup of coffee and a smile.

Ariel didn't buy it. "Well, that went about as well as I would have expected."

"What do you mean?" Colt asked, still looking pissed off and cranky.

"Nothing," Ariel replied, taking a step back from the hulking wall of muscle. She gave Michaela a wink as she took a sip of her coffee. Though, her face showed far more concern when she lowered her cup. "Maybe you should go get dressed, Colt. I'll keep Michaela company."

He glanced from one woman to the other, frowning. But eventually, he nodded. "Fine. But don't go anywhere."

Michaela saluted him with her left hand. "Aye-aye, Captain Underpants."

Ariel chuckled, hiding her grin behind her mug until he disappeared up the stairs with a huff. Then she got serious.

"We need to talk."

Michaela nodded, her eyes going to the screen door. Seeking her mate on instinct. "Yeah, I think we do."

Seven

The melodic lilt of his mate's voice soothed Phego's anxious mind, made him want to fall asleep as he lay in the dirt under the front windows of the cabin. The two women had been murmuring in the back bedroom for close to two hours, their voices hushed and words indecipherable, before they moved outside. Coffee cups in hand, smiles in place, Ariel and Michaela sat on the porch, talking more, exchanging histories and retelling old stories. Phego could sense their friendship, their bond. He could practically see the easy connection between the two.

Colt, the useless bodyguard who seemed to take great joy in smirking Phego's way every time he moved close to Michaela, was busy working in the kitchen. By the sounds of it, he was making himself something to eat. Phego couldn't remember him asking the ladies if they were hungry, which would have been what a real man did. At least, that's what Phego would have done if he had been the one making food. Especially for Ariel, who struggled climbing stairs and rising from a seated position due to the heaviness of the pup she carried. Phego did his best not to think about feeding his mate, about sliding his fingers in her mouth and letting her suck something sweet and delicious from them, about the way her thick, dark lips would look as they closed around that part of him. He refused to consider the way her brown eyes would lock on his as he cared for her, as he nourished her, as he treated her the way a woman should be treated. No, he couldn't think about that, not if he didn't want to have to deal with an erection in wolf form.

Phego stretched his front legs out, claws scraping across the dirt, achy from not shifting human in so long. Achy from a lot of things, like being around Michaela's scent so much. Like having such a beautiful woman to look at all day. Like the desire to bury himself inside her and bite down on her neck, claiming her, taking her as his.

He needed to stop thinking about the woman as his mate.

But as he told himself she wasn't his, Michaela laughed, the sound sending shock waves along his spine and amplifying his desires. For the first time since he saw her, he almost shifted human. Almost changed forms just so he could take her in with his other eyes, so he could reach out to touch her with his hand. So she could see exactly what the fates had offered up as hers. In his relaxed, dreamy mind-set, he had to admit that he wanted that. Wanted it enough that he almost gave up on his promise to himself to keep his distance and not give in to her charms—but Ariel's voice stopped him. She was his priority. His mission. His focus. His job was to keep her safe. Being in wolf form and not giving two strangers any leeway was the best way to do that.

So he stayed lupine, and he rested in the late-morning sun after another long, hard night patrolling the forest. And he fought every instinct he had, all the ones telling him to move beside Michaela, to brush against her, to rub his scent on her so the other male knew she was his. He planted himself in his dirt patch and held on, trying to grow roots strong enough to hold him back. Trying to do what was right.

As the ladies' talk turned to family and pack, to memories of things experienced long ago, so did Phego's thoughts. Michaela spoke joyfully about her situation, while Ariel sounded far more reserved. Understandable, really, considering her history. But it was Phego who locked down every muscle in his body at the memories of his youth, who grew cold at the visions playing out behind his eyes. Even the warmth of the day couldn't stop the chill of those thoughts.

Almost like a dream, flashes of the days leading up to what should have been his death flooded his mind. How his parents had been so closed off. How they'd practically refused to talk to him, his mother staring at the fireplace, his father looking out the window as he left to hunt each day. Phego had assumed they'd been fighting, the stress on the pack to hunt and survive the upcoming winter putting everyone on edge. He'd vowed to work harder, to find more prey and bring home plenty of food before winter came. He'd promised himself he would take care of them. But he'd only been a few hours into his last hunt for his pack when his brother had chased him down. He'd told Phego his parents needed him, that they had called for him to come home. Something they'd never done before. Phego had been sure something was wrong, though. He could sense it. Feel it. And even though he'd felt the danger pressing close, he'd followed his brother home…or to what he'd always thought of his home.

Not that time.

The slamming of the screen door yanked Phego back to the present, to the cabin in the woods. To the sense of danger once again blanketing the area. His wolf head shot up, his body tensed and ready to fight. Just as he'd been all those centuries ago when he'd walked into another little cabin he'd once called home. Fuck, he could still smell the fire and the damp, dank air of the valley they'd denned up in. And the blood.

"I'm going for a run," Colt said as he stomped across the porch. "Don't leave, don't do anything stupid, and if anything at all seems unusual, scream. I'll stay close enough to hear you."

Phego's lip curled in a silent snarl. Stupid? Both women were doctors, highly educated, and about the furthest thing from stupid he could imagine. Michaela must have nodded, as Phego didn't hear her speak her response. He did hear Colt start down the stairs and head toward the near side of the cabin for the woods, though. Interesting that he was leaving the women alone seeing as how he didn't know where Phego was or what he was doing. Was Colt setting them up? Seeking to meet with whatever Phego had sensed lurking in the forest? Scenting out possible hiding spots for future attacks? All possible. Phego didn't trust Colt, especially not when it came to the women on the porch.

Woman. His focus was Ariel, not Michaela. One woman.

Shaking off the last of his muddled, dreamy thoughts, Phego rose to his feet and slipped out of the bushes. Following Colt. Avoiding being seen by the women. When Colt made it to the tree line, Phego picked up his pace, letting the dirt and pine needles fall off his back as he padded across the grass. Ariel was laughing behind him again, reminding him of his goal on this mission. She was his priority, and he couldn't be distracted by anything else. He wouldn't go far, though. He just wanted to follow, to see, to make sure Colt wasn't doing anything other than running. To make sure he wasn't plotting against the women.

Woman. Ariel. One woman.

Colt's clothes lay folded underneath a tree at the edge of the forest, which meant he must've shifted. Good. Phego preferred hunting prey on four legs. He followed Colt's scent trail through the trees, along the path by the creek, and around toward the back of the property. Phego knew that route, had run it himself a million times. Colt definitely wasn't going far…yet.

Still, Phego searched his senses for any sign of something off. Something wrong or out of place. Whether unfortunately or not, there was nothing. No trace of whatever he felt in the woods the other night. No inkling of another person watching him, waiting for him. So Phego ran, ending up about thirty yards behind Colt. He stayed hidden in the trees, slipping in and out of the brush to avoid detection, while the other wolf ran ahead.

But as Colt's wolf reached the far corner of the property from the cabin, he stopped. Silent and still for reasons Phego couldn't determine. Phego crept close enough to see what was going on and tucked in behind a tree, waiting and watching. He didn't have to do either for long.

The bodyguard shifted from his wolf form, moving into his human skin in the blink of an eye. He turned, looking right to where Phego waited. Staring hard at the wolf who'd been following him.

"I know there's something you and Michaela aren't telling me," Colt said. He stood with his feet shoulder-width apart, his arms hanging at his sides, his fists clenched. The signs of a man about to fight. A boxer ready to exchange blows.

Phego walked out from behind the tree, staying in wolf form. Refusing to give in to the other man's need to confront someone. There was no way he was fighting this man. He didn't need to.

Colt growled when Phego didn't respond, when he didn't shift. The sound coming from the bodyguard was loud and gruff even in his human form, surprisingly so, but Phego's returning growl was more. Harsher, more violent, more threatening. It buried Colt's in volume, a fact that made the other man turn red in the face.

"She's coming back to our pack no matter what," Colt

spat, still growling, infusing his words with the rumble of his wolf in what Phego had to assume was supposed to be an intimidating way.

Phego wasn't intimidated by much of anything, especially not some overbearing wolf.

Colt took a step closer, then another. And another. Until he was less than ten feet away from Phego's wolf. "My job is to protect Michaela, to return her to our pack Alpha in one piece. Don't get any ideas about trying to get in the way of me doing just that."

Phego snarled, unable to stop the instinct to protect what was his. To respond to the threat this nothing of a man was throwing his way. Colt had just unknowingly stepped between a wolf and his mate. Even though Phego hadn't technically accepted Michaela as his, it was still a bad idea. No mated male would allow someone else to come between him and his female. That would be a fight to the death, and every shifter knew it. But Colt had no idea the two had mated, that they had a bond to one another. No matter how incomplete it was.

"Not going to answer me? Fine. I'm done with words anyway." The bodyguard shot Phego a cocky grin just before holding up his hand and bending his fingers in a come-hither motion. "Let's do this."

Colt shifted back to his wolf form, racing toward Phego before he was even completely on four legs. Brilliant. Phego hadn't planned on fighting, hadn't wanted to get into the politics of killing the bodyguard of Ariel's friend and midwife, but he wasn't about to back down from a direct threat. The fucker wanted to fight? Phego would fight...and he'd win.

The two wolves met in a crash of flesh, teeth, and claws, harsher and more brutal than even their scuffle the day before. Violent snarls broke the quiet around them, sending birds and prey animals scuttling. Neither man went for a kill move, though. Phego, because that wasn't part of his plan; Colt, probably unable to get at him. Phego was a great defender, able to ward off most one-on-one battles without difficulty. It was part of his skill set, part of his training as a Dire Wolf.

Still, Phego couldn't just let Colt show dominance over him in any way. He battled, defending himself against Colt's attack, until the smaller wolf made a mistake. One second, one twist in the wrong direction, and Phego pounced. He rolled Colt's wolf to his back, opening his mouth over his throat as if going for the kill. Clamping down and holding the bodyguard in place with his teeth. Colt froze, his body going almost limp, the instinct to survive by showing submission taking over. Self-preservation ruling his mind.

Before Phego could decide what he was going to do, how he was going to teach this fucker a lesson, a familiar sound broke through the haze of his rage. The cracking of a fallen branch under a heavy foot. Someone was close. Someone was watching. Again. Phego's head flew up, and Colt took the chance to scramble to his feet. Thankfully, the bodyguard had also heard the sound, so he didn't try to take advantage of the moment. Instead, he tensed, looking in the same direction Phego did. Waiting for some sort of sign, some sort of indication of what was out there. It came in the sound of one rock rolling against another. A soft ting that destroyed the stillness around them.

It might as well have been a starting gun going off.

Both wolves took off like a shot, racing toward the sound as if on a team. They even spread out naturally; ready to encircle their prey, ready to defend the women back at the cabin together. Working as one unit against a common threat.

But once again, the watcher was well hidden. Phego couldn't even get a solid scent trail on whatever was leading them through the trees. They were chasing shadows, racing after a deeper darkness through a forest most wouldn't have dared to enter. But even those shadows disappeared when they hit the riverbank, as did all traces of their intruder. No scent to follow, no sounds to chase after, and no more shadows.

Poof…gone.

Phego paced the water's edge, snarling. Raging inside at being tricked by the creature once more. That rage turned to dread, though, as his mind filtered through various scenarios for what the creature in the woods could have wanted. He wasn't there for kicks, wasn't there just to watch. Of that, Phego was certain. Was his presence on that day another ruse to be used as a distraction? To lead the men away from the women and leave them unprotected? Were they playing into his hand and putting Ariel and Michaela at risk?

Colt must've had the same thought at the same time, for both men turned toward the cabin, racing through the trees and heading for the women they were bound to protect. Their jobs were so similar, their duties so in line with one another. If he didn't hate the bastard, Phego could see being teammates in their fight against whatever seemed to be haunting his woods.

As expected, Phego was faster, his longer legs eating up the ground with every step. He tore through the woods in seconds, his mind oscillating between thoughts of Ariel and Michaela. Both needed protecting, both were important. Ariel because she was his mission, his pack, his friend's mate carrying the next generation of Dire Wolf. There was also Michaela. Beautiful, sexy, incredible…mate. As much as he still fought the connection, he couldn't let anything happen to her. Not that day, not ever. She deserved better, deserved protecting, deserved so much more than he could give her. A thought he couldn't deal with in that moment, so he tucked it away to unpack at a later date. A much later date.

Colt's wolf raced up beside Phego's, running alongside

him for a few steps. They glanced at one another, Phego assuming Colt was thinking the same thing he was by the regret in his dark eyes. They were idiots who weren't keeping those women safe as they were supposed to. No more. Phego would not be distracted. What was happening in the woods, the feeling that something was coming for them... That needed to be worried about. That had to be the priority. That was the threat to address first.

As Phego passed the bodyguard once more, his thoughts flew ahead of him. No one had ever trespassed on his property, not even the local hunters who took to the woods for food. No one had ever threatened his forest home before. How did the shadow in the woods find them? Who was he? Where had he come from?

But the biggest question, the one that ate at Phego and kept him in his wolf form more than anything else, was one he hated. One he couldn't help but think.

Did their guests, did Michaela and Colt, have something to do with the shadow? Had the shadow followed them? Or had they brought him as a distraction, a weapon, or a backup in case whatever their plan was failed?

Who was the shadow after, and why had it chosen that time to appear?

Eight

*M*ichaela was in the kitchen with Ariel when she first noticed it. The change in the air, a feeling of something darker, heavier, and more dangerous coming close. Something was off.

She pushed her senses out, bringing her wolf forward, needing the animal's much more sensitive eyes and ears as she evaluated her surroundings. The woods around the little cabin had grown quiet...too quiet. Everything had gone still in a way that made her wolf anxious.

Michaela took a deep breath, scenting the air, seeking any indication of what had her so on edge. Other than the fact that she was alone with Ariel. Or was she? Colt was still gone, off on his run through the woods, so he was no help. But Phego...

Not wanting to upset her friend, Michaela slipped silently toward the front of the cabin, fighting to keep her body language casual and her steps calm. Phego had been sleeping underneath the window earlier, hiding in his little spot he thought they didn't know about. If she was lucky, he'd still be there lying in the dirt in all his spotted glory, close enough to help if they needed it. Guarding them. But when

Michaela glanced outside, there was nothing but dirt and bushes underneath the window. Phego wasn't there. It was just her and Ariel, and the sense that something was wrong.

"Where's Phego?" Ariel said as she came to Michaela's side. She looked out the window as well, worry on her face, obviously sensing the same thing Michaela was.

"I don't know."

Ariel slid her hand over her baby bump in a move that screamed protection. "Where's Colt?"

Michaela waited, trying to figure out a way to answer that question without lying. She didn't want to scare her friend, but she refused not to tell the truth. There was no way she would break Ariel's trust. Not then, not when they could very well be heading into some sort of fight.

"I don't know," she whispered, still staring outside. Every hair on her body stood on end, every sense firing at once. This was bad. This was very, very bad. "They're both gone."

Ariel grabbed Michaela's arm, tugging her down the hall and toward the bedroom. "Hurry. The armory is back here."

Michaela followed, unable not to, sputtering, "You have an armory?"

Ariel opened the closet in her room and hurried inside, dragging Michaela with her. Hidden in the back corner was another door. A smaller door. One with a lighted display next to it the likes of which Michaela had never seen before. Ariel set her hand against the display and waited. A click sounded, then the display lit up with what looked like a number pad but without numbers. Ariel tapped buttons in a pattern Michaela couldn't comprehend, and another click sounded. This one deeper, harder. More solid.

The door popped open.

"What is this?" Michaela asked, staring in horror as Ariel began pulling weapons out of the closet.

"We need to protect ourselves."

"From what?"

Ariel grabbed an armful of guns and a huge, heavy-looking bag before heading back into the bedroom and tossing them on the bed as if they weren't deadly firearms capable of doing a hell of a lot of damage, even to a wolf shifter. "From whatever's coming for us."

Ariel began laying out the guns in a pattern much like a puzzle. Michaela could only stare, too stunned by her friend's knowledge of the weapons she had started loading to find words. At least until a crash sounded from the front of the cabin.

Michaela screamed and fell back a step as Ariel hoisted some sort of black weapon of death to her shoulder and aimed for the door. But it wasn't a stranger who came racing through—it was a familiar wolf, huge and terrifying in a whole other way. And spotted.

Ariel lowered her gun as Phego stormed into the room. He took up all the space, pushed all the air out of the room. And he came straight for Michaela.

He bumped into her, nudging her with his nose, sniffing and inspecting. Worrying over her flesh. Michaela dropped her hand and patted his head, an almost unconscious gesture. A way of seeking comfort in his presence. He was okay, safe, and there to protect them. That fact calmed her.

Eventually, Phego pushed her hand away and raised his head, looking Michaela right in the eye. She could almost feel his panic, his concern. For her.

"I'm okay," she whispered, trying hard to give him a smile. "Really."

And she was, until another crash broke the silence. This time, it was a naked, human man who raced into the room. One she knew.

"We need to go," Colt said as he lunged and grabbed

her elbow. Michaela yelped at the pinch, stumbling forward, making Phego growl in warning.

"No," Michaela said, pulling away from the man's hold. "I'm not leaving."

Colt glanced at Phego before leaning in, grabbing her again, pulling Michaela closer. "There was something out there in the woods. A threat of some kind, I'm sure of it. We need to get off this mountain and back to our pack before it gets more aggressive."

Michaela's eyes swept the room, taking in Phego as he stood with his hackles raised and his eyes swirling silver. Taking in Ariel, her gun by her side, looking fierce and intimidating. And scared. So very scared.

"No," Michaela said, shaking her head. "I'm not leaving. I need to stay with Ariel. I need to be here for the baby."

Colt growled. "Fine. She'll come with us."

Phego snarled in a way Michaela had never heard, the sound seeming to make the entire cabin tremble in fear. He stepped between Colt and Ariel, pushing the other man backward until he was forced out the bedroom door, his warning clear. She wasn't going anywhere. Neither woman was.

Ariel raised her chin in her own show of defiance, stepping closer to the spotted wolf guarding her. "I'm not going anywhere. Thaus told me to hole up here with Phego, that he'd be back for me before the baby came. I'm not leaving these woods without him beside me."

Colt focused on Ariel and opened his mouth to speak, to argue his point. Michaela, though, no longer cared about his words. Let him talk until he was blue in the face. She had more important things to focus on. Like the fact that Phego had moved closer again, nudging her hand until her fingers found his ears. Demanding contact with her in a way that made her heart flutter. There was something so sensual about petting the man in his wolf form, so intimate. So attention-stealing.

So utterly and totally enthralling.

Phego had her. Without a single word, without having shown her his human form, he had mesmerized every single part of her. And she was glad to be under his spell.

"We're not leaving," Michaela said, interrupting whatever Colt was saying. "Ariel and I will stay here and wait for Thaus to come back unless Phego tells us differently. You can choose to stay or go, but I'm in this for the long haul."

Phego nudged her leg with his hip, a move she took as accepting. As approving.

Colt glowered, his eyes angry, his lips twisted into a sneer. "Fine. But if anything goes wrong, it's on you." He turned his glare to the wolf at her feet. "And him."

Colt stormed off, leaving the three of them alone in the heavy silence. With all the guns.

"Please tell me you wanted to learn about these," Michaela said, her voice soft and her eyes locked on Ariel. "Tell me you didn't have to learn to defend yourself for another reason."

Ariel's face went white, and her hands began to tremble. "I wanted to learn, but because I had to. I didn't want to be weak again."

That was all Michaela needed to hear. She was across the room with the other woman in her arms in a heartbeat. "You were silent for a year, Ariel. I was so worried about you, but I hoped... Well, I guess my hopes failed. Are you okay?"

Ariel nodded into her shoulder, holding tight. "I am now. Thanks to Thaus and Phego and their pack. I'm doing a lot better than I was."

Michaela pulled out of the hold, eyes burning with unshed tears. "I won't push you to tell me what happened, but you can. I'm here for you."

Phego bumped his nose into Michaela's thigh, then rubbed his head against Ariel's arm.

"Guess he's there for you, too," Michaela said with a smile.

Ariel shrugged and wiped her eyes, regaining her composure. "He's my pack, my family. He'll always be there for me."

As Ariel began picking up the guns to load them back into the closet, as Phego padded out the door to lie in the hall like a guard dog, Michaela fought to hold back her smile. This little pack was so protective of each other, so tight-knit without being overbearing, it seemed.

This pack was one she'd like to be a part of, if only her mate would want her to be.

Nine

*P*hego spent the next three days constantly hunting, always tracking. Spending every hour possible searching for any sign of what or who had been in the woods. He patrolled all hours of the day and night, trading off with Colt when he simply couldn't run another step. Forcing himself to trust the bodyguard enough to close his eyes for a few stolen moments.

He barely slept, barely ate, instead, using all his time to sniff and hunt and investigate. He also remained wolf, refusing to shift to his human shape. Too afraid the danger would suddenly appear if he did, that he wouldn't be prepared. He'd promised Thaus that he'd protect Ariel, and while that mission stayed forefront in his mind, he couldn't help the fact that there was something else he saw as a priority. Something else he worried about. Someone else… and her name was Michaela.

But three days of hunting through the woods, endlessly searching for things he couldn't find, had left him with nothing. No sense, no tracks, no sign of who or what had been watching them. It was as if a ghost had come to the forest, as if someone or something had begun haunting them. Whoever it was, they were good at what they did, but he'd be better. He had to.

As he circled around toward the cabin on tired legs, beginning to wonder if too many days of being in wolf form had finally caught up with him, he finally spotted something. A sign. A single paw print, bigger than even his own, tucked underneath fallen leaves and disturbed undergrowth. Colt was smaller than he was, as was Thaus, which meant it couldn't be theirs. It had to be from another wolf, another shifter, someone who'd gotten too close to his wards.

But the strangest part, the fact that sent his mind spinning in a thousand directions, was that the print was completely out of place. The print was the only one. There wasn't a single track around it, not a dip in the earth to indicate additional steps. It was as if the beast had suddenly appeared in that spot, stood on a single foot, then disappeared.

Impossible.

But something not to be ignored.

Phego raced back through the clearing to the rear of the cabin, to the spot where he'd been keeping a set of clothes and a few extra things he might need in a hurry. Like his phone. He shifted as soon as he reached his hidden stash, staying in the trees. The physicality of the change from one form to the other was uncomfortable after so many days as a wolf, a fact that made him groan slightly. His muscles ached and his bones creaked, but he didn't even pause. He had work to do, and no irritations were going to hold him back.

Phego hurried into the old barn at the back of the property as he dialed, the phone ringing before he'd even crossed the threshold. He wasn't stupid or reckless enough to think he could handle everything with just Colt as backup, not anymore. He needed help. And there was only one person other than Thaus that he trusted to be available and show up in that moment.

"What's up?" Deus said the second he answered the phone. Phego practically sagged in relief at the tone of voice, knowing he had backup. Knowing he needed his Dire brother to keep Thaus' family safe and that Deus wouldn't let them down.

"Something's coming. Something big." Phego's voice was too rough, unused and almost broken. Too many days in lupine form had left his brain a little too scattered, his thoughts a little too wild, his instincts firing far harder than they should have been. He was still too much animal, still too far away from human to be around others. Deus would understand, though. He would know what was needed.

"Something big?" Deus paused, silent on the other end of the line. "Bigger than us?"

Phego closed his eyes and cracked his neck, picturing the footprint. The single piece of evidence that he wasn't losing his mind. "Yeah."

That time, Deus' voice sounded tougher. Darker. Less jovial. "Bear?"

"No. Wolf."

"Not possible. There *is* no wolf bigger than we are, especially not bigger than you. No wolf, no shifter, no canine or lupine of any sort. Even a werewolf wouldn't necessarily be bigger than us in full animal form."

"Luc may be bigger than me."

"He's in Alaska."

Phego took a breath, his mind racing, his thoughts still stuck in animal mode, though not enough that he couldn't see the picture becoming clearer. Not enough that he couldn't slide the puzzle pieces together. "Then it has to be another Dire."

Deus laughed a sarcastic cackle, mocking Phego, it seemed. "There are only seven Dires, and I'm looking at a screen now that shows where all of us are. You're the only one in that forest."

Something pricked at Phego's memory, something that sent a shot of adrenaline through his blood. A doubt. A story he'd heard come out of another continent centuries before. "But are there really only seven of us? Because the paw print was too big to be anything else."

Deus was silent for a long moment, only the sound of his harsh breaths coming through the phone. At least until he hissed a curse. "Fuck. I'll be there."

Phego nearly fell over backward in relief. Deus rarely emerged from what he considered his den, his apartment in the bustling and loud New York City. He was their tech guy, the man behind the screen, and he was damn good at his job. But he didn't like to leave his city, and he certainly didn't like to come to someplace so remote that he could possibly be forced to disconnect from his constant surveillance and internet watching. So the fact that he offered to rush to the wilderness told Phego exactly how nervous he should be.

"You're coming here?" Phego asked, needing that fact cemented in his brain.

"You bring me the possibility of more Dires and think I won't show up? Do you even know who I am?"

Phego almost smiled. Yeah, he knew. He knew well. Deus was the investigator, the one obsessed with finding reasons and connections, the spy. He was also addicted to being online. "We don't have internet here."

"I'll bring my satellite hookup. Hell, I'll bring an extra for you so you can finally move into the twenty-first century, old man."

Phego looked out a dirty, cracked window and toward the house, wishing to see the two women he guarded, wishing at the same time he wouldn't. If he spotted either one of them, saw their vulnerabilities, sensed his connection to them, it would just cement the reality of his situation. The possibility of loss. All the ways failure could come screaming into his forest. He couldn't even think about that—not while planning. Not until he knew another Dire had their six. One who wasn't as invested as…

"We can't call Thaus," Phego said, his voice flat. He deserved to know his mate was in danger, should have been the first phone call Phego made. But he was on a mission, one vital to the continuation of their very species as wolf shifters. Phego knew exactly what would happen if Thaus saw Phego's number on his phone.

Deus must've been on the same wavelength. "No, we can't. He'll either abandon the mission or stay and worry so much that he'll get himself in trouble. We can't risk the president that way."

Exactly Phego's fears. "Affirmative. Thaus is on blackout. Get here."

The clicking of keys in the background joined Deus' voice. "Already on it. I'll even call in Levi for secondary backup. Hole up for a couple of days, man. I'll get there."

"Sounds good." Phego hung up without another word, certain Deus would handle everything. The Dire knew where Phego lived, had seen him on GPS tracking maps for years. He could manage to make his way to the forest on the mountain. Of that, Phego was certain.

Still clutching his phone, Phego turned for the door, ready to shift back to wolf form. Ready to get back to work. But a shadow on the ground put that thought on hold. A shadow he'd know anywhere. One that didn't belong there.

Michaela stood in the doorway, watching him. A plate of food in her hands. Her eyes wide, lips parted in what could only be described as surprise.

Stunned and stunning all at the same time.

Phego had never seen a woman so beautiful, never been so entranced by something as simple as dark skin and hair coming together in a way that looked almost magical. She was gorgeous. And she was looking at him as if she'd seen a ghost.

"So you do shift human now and again."

Fuck, he was hard before her second word left her plush lips. Just looking at her brought his cock to attention. Just being close to her sent his wolf into a state of overpowering arousal. He'd already been too deep into his instincts, too far from his human side after spending so many days as his wolf. Seeing his mate looking at him like that…he was lost to the animal within. Totally and completely.

Michaela seemed a little over the edge as well. "You're so…hard."

Whether she meant his cock or his overall body didn't matter—she was right on both counts. Phego growled and stalked toward her, his wolf taking over. She was his mate, and he wanted her. Had he been in the right mind, had he been in his human thoughts, he would've stopped. Would have reminded himself of how he couldn't trust her. How she could be dangerous to him and Ariel. But his wolf was still in control, and the animal wanted her. Wanted to claim her as his. And, if he was being honest, so did his human side.

Michaela watched him, her eyes lighting up, the heavy scent of desire perfuming the air around her as she seemed to realize what was coming. What he wanted. He wouldn't take, though. His wolf didn't need to dominate her. That wasn't what he needed. He craved her consent. He wanted her willing, wanted her needing him just as much as he needed her.

"Mine," he growled as he reached her. He took the plate from her hand and threw it to the corner, ignoring the sound of breaking porcelain. Threw his phone, too. Michaela kept her eyes on his, breathing hard, nipples pebbled under her thin shirt. She wanted him. Whether she would let herself have him, he wasn't sure. But his wolf was speaking to hers. Seducing hers.

The animals within had already made up their minds.

Phego leaned over her smaller frame, still not touching, but close enough to feel her heat. To smell her arousal. "Mine. My mate."

Michaela shivered, her hands coming up to his chest. Her skin warm against his. He shivered from head to toe at the feel of her.

"My mate," she repeated, her voice breathy and filled with desire. Without any push from him, she rose to the balls of her feet, bringing her lips to his. The kiss was sweet, light and soft in a way Phego had never experienced. A perfect first kiss for just about anyone, but not nearly enough to satisfy his craving.

With a growl, he wrapped his arms around her waist and lifted her off her feet. Kissing her harder. Pulling her body against his. Trapping his cock between his stomach and her hips. She felt so good in his hold, so soft and warm as she melted against him. Willing. And that was everything to him. He wanted her that way. Wanted her begging for him. Wanted her screaming for him. He wanted to give her every bit of pleasure her body could take and have her asking for more.

Phego carried her over to an old worktable in the corner, sweeping his arm across the surface to rid it of the few tools and odds and ends resting there. Dust flew into the air as well, but he didn't care. He had one thought on his mind. One end goal made up of three parts.

To touch all of her.

To take whatever she was willing to give.

To claim his mate with his body.

Michaela gasped as he laid her back, spreading her legs around him and grappling for contact on his shoulders. "God, you're so big."

Phego couldn't hold back his grin, his hand slipping down to grab hold of his cock. To stroke it as he growled at the way her breath caught while she watched him. "Don't worry, baby. I'll keep this to myself for now."

He pushed her skirt up her long legs, letting his fingertips run along the silk of her skin. She moaned and moved against him, seeming to enjoy his touch. To want more. His actions were rougher than he'd have thought pleasurable to her, his wolf too out of control to be gentle. Luckily, Michaela didn't seem to mind. In fact, her panties were soaked, arousal evident even on her thighs. She liked this. Liked her male being in control and demanding. She wanted him that way.

And he was more than happy to give it to her.

Phego yanked the panties down her legs, exposing her pussy to his hungry gaze. Glistening, swollen with need, her flesh called to him. Sang to him. His mouth fucking watered at the thought of what was to come.

Michaela spread her legs wider, blatant in her need, leaning back on her elbows as if in offering. "Why are you stopping?"

"I'm not," Phego said, rubbing her thighs, pushing her apart even farther so he could see every intimate part of her. "I'm preparing myself for this. Your taste is going to ruin me."

She licked her lips and whispered, "Prove it."

Accepting the challenge from his mate, Phego dove in with fervor—licking, sucking, and spreading her with his thumbs so he could flick his tongue over her clit. Michaela moaned and arched her back, holding on to the edges of the table as she gave herself to him. As she encouraged him. But her submission wasn't enough, wasn't all that Phego needed. He wanted to own that pussy, to treat it so well she'd never forget the feel of his tongue inside her. To devour every fucking drop of her.

He hooked his arms under her hips and lifted, leaving her to rest on her shoulders and bringing her hips to his face so he could lick at every bit. So he could grip her ass with his fingers and attack her pussy with his lips and tongue. So he could destroy her as much as she was destroying him.

"Shit," Michaela said, a thick growl in her voice, thrusting her hips against his face as if riding his tongue. Such a hot fucking move for his needy little mate. She trembled at his touch, shook at every swipe of his tongue. Writhed with every nibble of her soft flesh.

And Phego ate it up.

He licked, kissed, and sucked every inch of her. Thrust his tongue inside to chase down every drop. Every taste. In that moment, with his mouth firmly latched on to her flesh and her taste all over his tongue, she was his. Completely. His mate. He would make her come. He would make her scream. He would make her crave him as he craved her. Her taste started a new addiction; the feel of her pussy on his lips something he could never get enough of. So he pushed, and he licked, and he tasted, and he worked her until she came. Until she arched her back and screamed *his* motherfucking name.

"Phego... Fuck," Michaela yelled, her entire body bowed with the force of her orgasm. Phego didn't let up, though, intent on giving her everything he could. He'd made his mate come so hard, she'd screamed for him. Didn't matter that it was only on his tongue and not his cock. He did that; he gave her that pleasure. And fuck, did he want to do it again.

But Michaela had plans of her own. As she came down, as her body relaxed and her trembling muscles stilled, she grabbed Phego's arm and yanked him on top of her. Trapped him between her thighs.

"Take me," she said, her eyes locked on his, her words harsh and demanding. "Fuck me now and claim me as yours."

He couldn't tell her no.

Ten

Michaela could barely catch her breath, could barely see straight enough to focus on Phego's face. Her body burned, alive for the first time, her instincts firing jointly between her human and wolf in a pattern that heightened her senses. The moment had come—she was giving herself to her mate. In a dusty old barn on a rickety workbench, she would claim and be claimed. There'd be no going back from this, no second chances or do-overs. There was no divorce in the shifter world, no annulments or separations. Once they joined one another, once his body and blood mixed with hers, they'd be one. A mated pair.

She couldn't wait.

Michaela grabbed Phego's shoulders, pulling him closer, wrapping her legs around his thighs so his heavy cock slid through where she was so wet for him. His skin was so soft and smooth. It was a total contrast to the hard muscles cording their way beneath it. She could have lay there and done nothing but explore him with her fingertips for hours. Could have…but that wasn't part of his plan, it seemed.

Phego climbed up her body, kneeling above her. His gray eyes locked on hers, his sharp jawline clenched in need. With his white-blond hair cut so short and the scruff of a day's stubble dusting his lower cheeks and chin, he seemed ready to go to war…for his home or her body. He was brutal in movement and appearance just as she'd expected, and she loved it. Found herself attracted to the man in ways she hadn't anticipated. From the dips and planes of his abdomen to the bulky width of his shoulders, he was an education in musculature and the male form. That fact spoke to her, aroused her with all that chained-up strength. He could crush a person if he wanted to, could destroy any enemy with only his body. But he wouldn't. Not her, at least. He wasn't gentle by any stretch, but he wasn't cruel. Wasn't out to hurt her. The opposite, really. He'd been rough because she'd liked it, had demanded because she'd needed him to. He fulfilled her every desire…almost.

Phego dropped his weight on her, pinning her down, teasing her with his closeness and his position. Pushing her to the point of unfettered control. She could feel the cold, wet spot she'd left on the table, smell her arousal on Phego's face. Sense how close he was, how hard, how much he needed.

She needed, too.

She wanted him inside her. Wanted him in a way she'd never felt for another partner before. This wasn't just sex. It was weighty and meaningful, powerful. This was fate and spirits and souls all tied together. This was the start of her forever.

"Please," she murmured, writhing under him. Seeking more.

Phego rocked on top of her, sliding the tip inside her pussy, groaning long and low as he trembled with what had to be restraint. "We shouldn't do this."

"Yes, we should." Michaela clawed at his shoulders, running her nose along his as she stole his breath. Damn, she wanted to kiss him. Wanted to feel those thick, pink lips on hers. Wanted him to fuck her mouth with his as he slid deep inside her. He was just so beautiful in his own way—his short, light hair and his icy gray eyes the only soft spots on his otherwise hard as hell body. Harsh was a good descriptor for him. Harsh and rough. And hers. All fucking hers. And she wanted to make sure he knew that.

She bit him. Not a claiming bite—not yet—but enough to remind him of what they were about to do.

Phego grunted and dropped his head to her shoulder, leaning on his elbows and pressing her into the table. Covering her. Touching every bit he could.

"Want more," he said, his words rumbling with his growl. "Want to feel you come on my cock."

Michaela gasped, shaking. Already so close. "So make me."

Phego groaned, the sound almost a wail as he moved like a man possessed, a man fighting an instinct. Michaela wasn't sure if that instinct was to push forward or back away, though. So she waited, her arms around him, running her palm up and down his spine as he growled against her. Gave him the chance to decide one way or the other.

And decide he did.

With nothing more than a hissed *fuck*, Phego jerked his entire body forward, thrusting inside her in one push. Spreading her wide with his hips between her thighs and owning her body. She clawed his back, fingers digging deep as he moved in and out, deeper on each push, hitting places inside her that had never been hit so hard before. Setting off nerves that had only just come alive.

When he grabbed her leg, when he pulled her knee up over her shoulder to push in farther, spread her wider, she almost screamed.

"Fuck yes," she cried, biting down on his shoulder to keep from chanting his name. He roared and moved faster, harder, the old worktable rocking underneath them. Savage and unrelenting, he fucked her like a man possessed. Like a man who couldn't get enough. And still, she knew he was holding back. Felt it.

"I don't trust you," he said between thrusts, clinging to her. His words refuted by the way his body responded to her every breath, her every moan and shiver. Michaela arched into him, craving more touch, pressing her body into his so he pushed against her clit on every swell forward.

"I know you don't." She whined as he hit just the right spot, his body curling over hers, the base of his cock rubbing along her clit with every slide. "You'll learn to. I'll prove myself to you."

He grunted and pulled her leg higher, straightening it, practically putting her into a half split underneath him. The position was so filthy, the noises their bodies made as they came together so fucking debauched, she almost felt embarrassed. Almost, but his cock inside her felt too good, and his body slamming into hers was too enticing. There was no room in her mind for propriety or embarrassment. There was only her and him and every titillating second of what they were doing together. Every snap and grunt and filthy suck of flesh on flesh.

As Phego snarled into her neck, pressing his teeth against her skin, she lost all capability of thought and speech. Her body screamed for him, every nerve ready to explode. The pressure built in her gut, the need to let go. To release. To fall over that cliff of ecstasy and give herself to the man inside of her. Phego was close as well, if his own coordination was any indication. Harder, deeper, faster…everything coming together, every press becoming a circle of movement dragging her soul around and around and around until there was nothing else. Nothing left. Until, with one final thrust and a roar that shook the windows, he came inside of her. That sensation, that wet heat from his release, sent her flying as well. Sent her muscles spasming and her mouth falling open as she clenched around him in an orgasm that spread throughout her entire body. Cradling him as she milked every drop. As she rode out every pulse.

Phego collapsed on top of her, breathing heavy, cock still inside her. Still hard, from the feel of him stretching her. She didn't know if she had it in her for another round, but it didn't matter. Not after the barn door flew open and Colt ran inside.

"What the—" Colt stood in the entryway, staring at them. Wide-eyed and obviously in shock. Michaela didn't even have time to pull away, to cover herself with more than the man on top of her, Phego not having time to pull out of her before the bodyguard shifted to wolf. Colt growled and snarled, directing his hate to her mate, whom he didn't know about. Didn't have any clue that they were connected in any way other than the physical. And he wasn't giving her time to explain. There was nothing she could do, but still, she tried.

"Colt, no—"

But it was too late. Phego sprung off of her, shifting almost in midair. Leaving her cold and alone…and afraid. For her, for him, and for Colt. The two wolves attacked one another a mere few feet away, teeth and claws and snarls all coming together in a picture that turned her stomach. The fighting was ugly and violent, brutal in a way Phego hadn't been with her. Bloody from the onset and definitely heading toward deadly. Michaela couldn't let the fight go on. Couldn't stand to see either man hurt.

She lunged toward them, ignoring her tattered clothes and missing panties, the burn of her muscles between her legs or the coldness dripping down her thighs. She had one job, one focus, and that was to plead with the males to stop and listen to her.

But as she jumped off the counter, her skirt caught on the front edge. The tug, the pressure backward, and then giving away before she adjusted, sent her flying face first toward the floor. Right into the fight. Directly between the two. She wasn't sure which male caught her, wasn't sure which one slashed at just the right or wrong moment, but someone had their claws in her flesh before she hit the ground. She screamed, pain flaring bright. Skin and muscle and even bone burning under the attack.

Before she hit the ground, before she could even twist to see the damage, Phego had her in his arms. He raced out the door in human form, heading for the cabin, carrying her.

"I've got you," he said as he hit the porch. Michaela couldn't answer him, too busy fighting back tears as pain racked her body.

Ariel met them in the kitchen, looking far more startled than Michaela had ever seen her. "What happened?"

"She got in the way," Phego said, setting Michaela down on the couch. Ariel rushed over with a towel, placing it on her shoulder where the slashes were the deepest.

"Go get her doctor bag from upstairs," Ariel said, sliding into doctor mode in the blink of an eye. "These will knit together; what we're going to have to make sure of is that they do so correctly."

Phego's stomping footsteps receding across the floor were his only answer. His absence hurt, tightening around her chest like a steel band. Shifters healed quickly; in fact, there wasn't much that could kill them. That didn't mean they always healed in the best way. Broken bones were broken bones, and if they didn't line up properly, there were long-term issues. Same with muscles, tendons, and cartilage. Someone would need to help hold her together as her flesh knitted into one piece. Someone would have to help her. She had a feeling it wouldn't be Phego.

Colt had come in through the back door by the time Phego came downstairs. He surveyed the scene with something akin to disgust on his face. "I can't believe you did this."

Michaela assumed the words were meant for her, but it was Phego who answered. "It's my fault. She's not to be blamed for anything."

"Why are we even arguing over fault? Since when is there fault in something as natural as sex?" Ariel huffed, pressing Michaela's skin together, frowning at the cuts. "And if there is fault to be found, it's on both of you. This is what you get when you refuse to deal with a new mate bond."

Michaela tore her eyes away from her mate to take in her bodyguard and packmate. Colt stood frozen, barely blinking, looking stricken. "You're mated to *him*?"

Michaela refused to lie, refused to allow anyone to diminish her bond to her mate. "Yes. We're mated."

But the confidence behind her words deflated as Phego stared down at her. Saying nothing. Doing nothing.

At least, not until he turned away.

Eleven

Phego stayed by Michaela's side all night, refusing to abandon her even for a moment. The guilt of knowing he'd hurt her, that his claws had damaged her flesh, swamped him, freezing him in place. Leaving him useless and unable to function beyond simple existence.

Ariel stayed as well, pressing on her friend's torn flesh to hold the edges together properly, a voice of calm and reason in a sea of doubts and fears. Colt, the bodyguard, came and went. Checking on Michaela every so often before heading back outside. He kept his phone in his hand, obviously calling someone or texting. Phego couldn't focus enough to concentrate, to listen in, though the man's face was pale and filled with anger whenever he appeared. Whatever was going on with him, it wasn't good.

"She'll be okay," Ariel whispered once Colt had again left the room. She checked the wound for what had to be the hundredth time that night, lifting the bandage to look underneath. To his relief, the skin appeared almost completely closed, though the dark red tracks of claw marks still screamed from the pale flesh. Claw marks that were absolutely his fault. He knew it, had felt the slash as it happened. Hadn't been fast enough to stop himself once he'd realized who he'd hit.

And that fact ate at him almost as much as his deeper, darker worries. "I can't trust her."

Ariel sighed, looking tired and frustrated. "Yes, you can. She's your mate."

Mate. A silly word. One he'd examined in his head for so long and from so many different angles that it no longer made sense. As if it ever had. "I don't even know what that means...to me. How that could be."

"It means you can trust her, and it could be because the fates deemed her your match." Ariel covered Michaela's shoulder once more, pulled the blanket up tight around her neck, and turned her steely glare on Phego. "She's healing. That shoulder will be fine in a few hours. She might not even have a scar, but she will have a broken heart if you don't pull your head out of your ass."

He wanted to say something, anything, but he was speechless. Ariel knew he'd been the one to do the damage. Knew his claws had caused Michaela so much pain. Yet, she was still trying to help them be together somehow.

"It doesn't matter. Some intangible bond shouldn't matter."

Phego had never seen Ariel look so angry.

"She's your mate, the other half to your soul. She's meant to be with you, just as you're meant to be with her. How can you be so flippant about this situation when you've been alone so long? How can you turn your back on her when you've seen the joy Amy, Sariel, Charmeine, and I bring to your brothers? Do you not care? Are you simply so dead inside that you can't accept the fact that someone could care about you in any way?" Ariel asked, imploring him with her words before rising to her feet slower than she would have a few hours ago. "She is the only mate you will ever get in however long your life is, Phego. That's not something to throw away. *We* are not something to throw away. You'll regret it if you do."

Ariel left without another word, leaving Phego alone with his sleeping mate and his swirling thoughts. *Mate.* Such a thing had never truly crossed his mind as a possibility. Had never been something he'd wished for, hoped for, or wanted. He was too scarred, too blocked off. Too set in his ways. Too untrusting and scared, if he was honest. And Michaela deserved better.

Still, he couldn't help but reach for her, to quell his need with the feel of her skin under his fingertips. A light stroke of her cheek was all he allowed himself, though. Just the one. He needed to keep control of his wolf. Keep control of himself. He couldn't risk hurting Michaela again, and he definitely couldn't risk anything distracting him from the danger lurking around them.

Phego must've fallen asleep at some point because the next thing he was aware of was a warm quilt under his face and the soft stroking of fingers in his hair. He jerked up, meeting Michaela's sleepy eyes. The room was still dark, night hanging heavy around them, but he could see her face. Her expression. The slight smile she wore loosened his muscles, and the intimacy of the blanket of darkness around them steadied his soul.

"Hi," she said. Such a simple statement preceding so many difficult decisions. But first…

"Are you okay?"

"Yeah. Are you?"

"Yes." But was he? Would he ever be okay? A week ago, he would've said he was fine. Everything was great. Life was as it should be. But right then, post meeting Michaela, after feeling and tasting and giving in to her, he wasn't sure if anything would ever be okay again.

And Michaela must have somehow sensed that. "You don't trust me."

He hated hurting her, but he had to be honest. Had to tell her the truth. Even if it caused more confusion. "I don't know if I *can* trust."

Her eyes stayed locked on his, voice firm as she said, "Yes, you do."

Phego couldn't answer her, couldn't risk seeing the pain on her face when he said what he truly thought. When he announced his confusion and reluctance. He never should have been alone in the barn with her. He never should have claimed her with his body when he was so torn over her very presence. He should have been a better man, a stronger one. For her.

Michaela sighed, sagging into the pillows, suddenly looking so small and defeated. "Can we at least try?"

Phego dropped his head, unable to look her in the eye as he thought of a way to answer that question. Try? Try what…try not to kill one another? Try to learn to trust, even after centuries upon centuries of failing on his part? What was the point in trying? What was it she wanted from him?

But the only words that came to him were the wrong ones. "Someone has been in the woods around the cabin."

Michaela startled, her eyes going wide. "What?"

"Someone has been stalking the house. Colt and I have both sensed them, but they leave no trail. They're like a ghost, a potentially dangerous one."

Michaela's lips turned down in a frown, her face hardening with something close to anger. "I would never risk my friend. I would never risk the baby. Whatever is out there, it's not because of me."

Phego sighed and stood, pulling away from her. Forcing his feet to head toward the door. "I want to believe you—"

"Then do it. Put a tiny bit of faith in me as your mate. Try, for me."

He swallowed hard, knowing he was an asshole for what

he was about to do. Hating himself for purposely causing her harm. But he had a mission, a job to do, a promise to keep. And he needed to focus on the surroundings and not on the woman lying on the couch if he was going to accomplish his task.

"I can't. I don't know how."

Phego didn't stick around to hear her response. He hurried out of the room, rushing outside and into the night. Into the hell where he belonged.

Twelve

For days after the accident, after the time in the barn that Michaela refused to think about but couldn't get off her mind, Phego put space between them. He hadn't disappeared, hadn't run off and completely abandoned them. He stalked through the woods and lurked in the shadows, always watching. Always hunting, it seemed. At least in wolf form. He was around even though she hadn't seen his face since he left her with those cutting words after she begged him to try for her.

I don't know how.

Painful, more so because he'd left right after that and hadn't spoken to her since. Still, she felt him, sensed his eyes on her as she did the most mundane of activities outside. Hiding and avoiding her even as he watched her from a safe distance away. Refusing to come inside unless Ariel called for him.

Michaela would like to have said it didn't bother her, that his refusal to accept her as his mate for more than just a moment of physical pleasure was nothing. But the fact that he'd joined with her in such an intense, intimate way and then practically abandoned her hurt. That hurt a lot.

During the day, she stayed busy with Ariel—exercising, examining, making sure the woman was relaxed and fed so she'd have the strength once the time came. During the day, Ariel tried to mend fences she hadn't broken.

"He's not always like this," Ariel said the first morning after the barn, her eyes soft, her lips turned down in a frown. "He has a history—"

"One he would tell me himself if he wanted me as his mate."

And so it went. Ariel would slip in little bits about Phego, and Michaela would try to redirect her. It didn't always work. Ariel managed to get across that Phego's family had tried to have him killed for reasons no one seemed to know, that he barely trusted his Dire Wolf pack, or brothers, as they called one another. That he'd stayed right beside Michaela while she'd rested and recovered from the barn incident. All things that melted a little of the hardness from Michaela's damaged heart. But then she'd hear him, feel him close by, and she'd grow angry once more. And sad. She was always so sad.

But during the bright hours of the day, Michaela could ignore her draw to Phego. In the dark was a different story. At night, she would hear him in the woods, running laps around the property. Never straying too far from the cabin. Never leaving the small area of forest around them. That hurt as well. He trusted her only enough to stay within hearing distance. Never enough to completely leave Ariel alone with her. Michaela understood it at the same time that she hated it. Ariel was his friend's mate, a part of his pack, and someone he was sworn to protect. And Michaela? Well, Michaela was apparently an interloper. A threat. A possible diversion from the real danger waiting for them all.

She was also mate to a man who didn't want one.

Colt continued to sleep on her floor, refusing to leave Michaela's side for more than a few minutes at a time, unlike the man the fates had chosen for her. But Colt wasn't so much protective as hyped up on fear. Nervous. An uncomfortable energy to be around, especially for Ariel. Especially when Michaela wanted to sleep.

She wished the man in her room every night was Phego. Wished he would come to check on her. The most selfish part of her, the wolf within her, wished he would watch over her instead of Ariel. But her wishes never came true, and she was left with Colt looming over her every minute of the day.

A frustrating proposition.

On the third morning after *the barn incident,* as she had begun calling it in her own mind, Michaela woke up in the wee hours of the morning. The sun hadn't even broken the horizon, yet she went from out cold to completely conscious and motivated to move in a breath. Anxious and ready to do *something.* What, she had no idea, but she felt it. The need for action. The need to get up and start her day right that second. So she did.

Michaela crept out of her room, sneaking past Colt with practiced ease and slipping out the door. Avoiding every creaky step, she headed downstairs, giving in to her need to be…somewhere other than where she was. The pull inside of her led her to the front door, enticed her to open it. To step out onto the porch. She closed the door behind her, not wanting the others to hear. To worry.

Wrapping her arms around herself to ward off the chill, Michaela stood in the eerie darkness. Waiting. Listening. For what, she had no idea. There was nothing out there. No sign or mate, no person waiting with all the answers. There was only dark, only black. Only one crazy woman standing on the porch of a cabin in the woods in the cold mountain air without a coat.

Until suddenly, she wasn't alone anymore.

The feeling of being watched, of being joined, crept up on her. Her wolf perked up, a warning growl whispering through her mind. Michaela sensed Phego nearby, knew he'd been sleeping outside. The sensation coming from the watcher felt different than when Phego was close, though. Felt somehow rougher. Scarier. Perhaps it was being alone in the dark with him or the quiet hour they were in. Whatever it was, it didn't matter. She was desperate to talk to Phego instead of talking about him.

"I miss you," she whispered into the dark. She sensed him slip closer, the soft sound of something creeping toward her through the woods giving her a sense of peace and courage that buried the instinctual fear it also aroused. Knowing he could hear her even if she couldn't see him, she let the words come unbidden. Unfiltered. Raw.

"I wish we could figure this out. I know being mated, especially to a stranger, can take some getting used to. I've seen the awkward stress of a new couple joining throughout my years in my pack, but we can attempt to move past that if you'll let us. We both have to at least be willing to try." She ducked her head, tears burning the edges of her eyes, her voice weak as she murmured, "I'm willing to try. You said you didn't know if you wanted to, but I want to. Do you? Will you try for me? Will you try with me?"

The only response was a deep, throaty growl from out in the darkness. A dangerous one. A warning. That wasn't the growl of a mate to his partner, not the growl of a man to the woman he wanted, even if that desire was only physical. That growl was a warning to an enemy, a threat of violence and anger. And it broke her.

With nothing but a shattered heart and a sudden fear of the man she'd been mated to, Michaela spun and hurried inside. Tears streamed down her face and she gasped repeatedly, her breaths coming hard and raspy. She wished she hadn't gone outside. Wished she hadn't said what she did. Not knowing was far better this burning in her chest, this ripping of her heart. Better than the agony of finally understanding Phego didn't want her at all. That he hated her. That he saw her as dangerous even when—

"Where were you?"

Michaela jumped, eyes going wide and heart slamming in her chest. The shock of that voice so close, so human, pulling her up short. And making her brain short-circuit a little. "How did you get in here so fast?"

Phego stood in the kitchen, a glass of what looked like orange juice in his hand. Clothes missing, skin dirty, he had the look of a man who'd just shifted human after a long go as a wolf. He had the look of a man...period.

He stared at her in what could only be pure confusion. "What are you talking about?"

Michaela shook her head, taking a moment to catch her breath and wipe away her tears before pointing toward the front door. "I was just talking to you out there..."

Her mouth fell open, her words dying on her tongue as realization slammed into her. Whatever was outside, whatever beast she'd poured her heart out to, wasn't her beast. It wasn't Phego. Colt was still upstairs; she'd left him sleeping on the floor. Ariel was down the hall, the pregnant woman unable to shift due to her heavy burden. Which meant something else was out there. Something in the woods. Something that had drawn her out of the house with a yearning, some sort of Alpha power. Something that had gotten close enough to have snatched her if it had wanted to.

A fact that Phego must have realized at the same time she did.

His face went hard, the glass nearly shattering as he tossed it into the sink. "Get upstairs, take Ariel with you, and wake up Colt."

Michaela moved without thinking, responding to orders as any good pack animal would. But she only took two steps toward Ariel's room and then stopped. Phego was heading outside, heading into the dark of night. Heading out to hunt whatever it was she'd sensed out there. He was rushing into danger to protect them all. Something about that, some sense of dread for his future, set her on a different path.

She rushed to him, slamming into his body before he could reach the door. Wrapping her arms around his neck and pulling him down to her so she could plant her lips on his. And he came with her, accepted her, sought her lips as much as she sought his. The kiss was explosive, wild and untamed. Completely out of control. Completely perfect in its feralness. Phego matched her intensity, his arm slipping around her waist and his hand dropping down to her ass. Grabbing her tight, holding on. His tongue stroking hers with deep, long passes. His growl rumbling against her chest, the sound familiar and right and so fucking sexy. That was the growl of a mate. The growl of a man aroused by his woman. That was a growl of hope that they still had a future. Somehow. Some way.

Michaela broke apart from him with a moan, licking his taste from her lips and shaking with desire. Needing so much more but knowing there was no time. Knowing she might not ever get more if Phego kept throwing himself into the danger. Or if he simply refused.

"Please," she whispered, clutching him tight, her fingers practically embedded in his neck. "Please try."

Phego didn't respond with words. Didn't give her platitudes or possibilities. He simply held her tighter, nuzzling into her neck to place a small bite at the base. A move of claiming. A move of want. A move that said more about their possible future than he could.

"I have to go." His voice rumbled against her skin, and

his arms tightened around her once more as if he didn't want to leave her. It was a small thing, that squeeze. A tiny signal of his needs, of his desires. A brief moment of acceptance she'd take as hope.

Michaela clutched him hard, knowing this could be their last embrace. Knowing he was in danger. That they all were.

"Stay safe," she whispered before taking two steps back and dropping her arms from around him. Letting him go. Knowing he had to be the soldier to protect them. Still hating it.

Phego gave her one last look, a deep, intense stare that said so many wonderful, hope-filled things…

And then he was gone.

Thirteen

Phego raced outside, the taste of Michaela's kiss still on his lips. His body craved her, his mind focused on her. On them. On fixing things. He had been such an idiot to avoid her, and he'd come inside to try to find a way to talk to her. To lay his past on the line and hope for a future. He wanted her, wanted every part of her. He had planned to drag her sexy ass back to the barn for some more privacy, but the creature in the woods had shattered that idea.

But she'd spoken to him, kissed him. Had embraced him with one of those hugs he'd coveted. And he'd loved every second of it. He wanted more. Once he had rid the woods of whatever had been lurking there lately and Thaus came back for Ariel, he was going to show Michaela how much he wanted. Prove to her that he could be a good mate if she had patience with him. But first, he had a lurker to deal with.

To kill.

He couldn't fail his mate, who'd been in danger outside while he hadn't been paying attention. While he'd been too deep into his thoughts of missing Michaela, wanting her, craving her touch—a fact that would eat at him until he made it up to her. He couldn't fail Ariel either. Whatever was watching them from out in the woods had gotten braver. Dared to move closer. The fucker had totally invaded Phego's territory and challenged him on his own turf. He couldn't let that happen.

Phego practically flew through the trees in a loop, using the cabin as a center point. Working slowly farther away to try to sniff out the trail of the lurker. Colt joined him at some point, spiraling in the opposite direction, the two unconsciously working as a hunting party on the search for a scent trail.

But when Phego found it, when he finally scented the beast that had been watching them, the force of the surprise it threw nearly knocked him to his ass. The trail left behind was the scent of a Dire, but not one of his brothers. Not one of his pack. Familiar in a way that almost made him tremble. The scent tugged at a memory, pulling hard at the darkness of Phego's youth. This was an old Dire, one he knew, one he had history with, which was impossible. There were only seven Dires left...one pack of them. His pack. Bez, Levi, Mammon, Thaus, Deus, Luc, and him. They were all that was left of their breed. That scent, that creature, was not part of their pack. Was not supposed to be alive.

Something was definitely wrong on a total shitstorm level.

Phego shook off his shocked stupor and ran faster, scenting more, yipping to let Colt know he was on the trail. His nose dropped to practically touch the ground, his steps quickened and grew lighter. He would track the fucker down, he had to. He needed to figure out what the hell was going on and how to protect his pack from it. His pack, including Michaela.

The beast had taken a direct path deeper into the woods,

skirting the creek for a solid fifty yards before turning toward it. Disappearing into the water at one point and hiding its scent beneath the ripples. That creek was an offshoot of a larger, stronger river not too far away. Phego could sniff up and down both banks, seeking the place where the creature had left the creek for dry ground. Could, but he took a chance and followed the smaller waterway toward the river instead. That had to be where the creature had gone. Probably. Because that's what he would do; what a wise old Dire would do. Use the rushing water to mask his scent so he could escape.

And come back to fight another day.

But before he could reach the river itself, the sound of an animal approaching shattered his concentration. He spun in the darkness, teeth bared, hackles raised. Ready to fight. But the wolf who rushed after him was one who was familiar. One who was welcomed. One who wasn't a bodyguard.

"What's going on?" Phego asked the second he shifted to his human form.

Dire brother Deus shifted human as well, rising to his full height on two legs. Heavy with muscle, far more body builder in type than the other Dires, though shorter, Deus stood in the dark, looking like an evil spirit hunting its prey. Piercing Phego with his sharp eyes.

"I just got out here a few minutes ago and heard your hunting yip, so I decided to follow you," he said, his voice deep but quiet. The sound of a man who knew there could be ears overhearing what he had to say. "I saw Ariel for a second, though she looked pretty heartbroken I wasn't Thaus. Saw the other shewolf as well. You know, the one who smells a fuck of a lot like you right now."

Phego couldn't concentrate on the accusation in those words. Couldn't worry about Deus finding out about him and Michaela at that moment. He couldn't even let himself think of Michaela at all, even though she was always on his mind. "Smell that."

Deus raised an eyebrow but followed Phego's pointed finger, leaning down to sniff the trunk of a tree where the scent he'd been chasing had rubbed off. A mistake by the beast Phego had been hunting. Deus jerked back at the scent, his eyes wide enough to see even in only the subtlest moonlight.

"Dire."

"Right," Phego said with a nod. "Not one of ours, either."

A chill flew down Phego's back, the sense of incoming danger. But relief was there as well in the form of his brother. His Dire packmate. Deus would help protect the land and the cabin. Would protect the women with his life, just as Phego would. They would figure this out as a team. A unit. A family.

In fact, Deus took a look at Phego's face, probably assuming exactly where his thoughts had gone, and grunted. "Let's hunt."

Phego shifted first, falling to four feet and shaking out his fur. Deus followed, then set the pace as they tracked their prey. Running through the trees and over rocks, following the creek as it headed toward the river. And just as Phego had expected, when the creek hit the river, the scent trail appeared on the banks then disappeared back into the stronger, wider water.

Each wolf took to the river, sniffing the opposite bank in hopes of locating where the beast had come out, but it was no use. The scent was gone. As was their prey.

Phego walked out of the river on the side of his property, not even leaving the bank before he shifted back to human. "Shit. This fucker has been tracking us for days, but he's ghosted every time I get a bead on him. I just can't nail him down."

Deus shifted as well, his pale skin almost glowing, a

heavy frown pulling down his brow. "We need to get back. If there's one, there could be more."

"I don't think so. I think it's one man, one shifter."

Deus cocked his head. "One Dire Wolf?"

"How is that possible?" Phego asked, knowing there was no answer. The only way to know, the only way to truly find out, would be to catch the enemy alive. Which, if that creature was like his own Dire brothers, was going to be a hard task to accomplish.

"This is insane," Deus said as they headed back toward the cabin. "What the fuck could it be?"

Phego followed him through the trees, his mind spinning. Those long-forgotten memories pulling at him. "I don't know, but we have to figure it out. It's familiar to me."

Deus nodded, as if he agreed. As if he too felt that familiarity. "Let's make sure the women are safe, and then we can start to work this puzzle out. We'll unravel it. No matter what."

Phego nodded and shifted wolf, more comfortable on four legs. Faster too. He had a mission to accomplish, a shewolf to keep safe, and a mate to check on as well. Time was of the essence.

Fourteen

Ariel didn't look good. In fact, in Michaela's opinion, she looked as if she was going into labor. Not next month or next week, not even tomorrow. Soon. Sooner than they'd planned. Sooner than they were ready for.

"Why don't you relax for a few minutes?" Michaela asked, fighting the urge to hover. To walk with her as the woman paced the length of the living room and back. "We can go upstairs, and you can lie down for a bit."

But Ariel would not be swayed. Over and over, the pregnant shewolf walked while Michaela waited and watched. And worried. The friend in her wanted to commiserate with Ariel, to give her false promises that Thaus would make it back any second to reunite with his family and be there when his first child was born. The midwife in her knew better. Especially when her patient hissed and pressed her hand against her lower back.

"Ariel, please. Try to relax."

The shewolf shook her head and continued her trek,

pausing every few minutes to close her eyes at what Michaela could only guess was the pain of those first contractions. "I can't relax. What's happening out there? Why aren't they back yet? Why isn't Thaus here yet?"

All good questions. All questions Michaela couldn't answer. "They'll be back. They'll all be fine, as will we."

Ariel saw through her, knew those words were nothing but a platitude. As close to a lie as Michaela was willing to offer. "You don't know that."

Michaela had nothing to say to that. Especially not when Ariel paused again, closing her eyes, this time catching her breath and rocking in a way that showed her pain. Three minutes since the last one. Michaela watched with practiced eyes, noting every tell of a pregnant woman in labor. Marking time as she had done thousands of times before. Experienced enough to know her friend was having back labor pains, which meant the baby could be in the wrong position for what was about to occur.

"Ariel," Michaela said, keeping her voice calm. Knowing the shewolf was already on edge. "Why don't you lie down for me? Rest your legs while I check the baby. You're going to need your strength."

Ariel pinned her with an angry glare, her understanding of what Michaela was trying to do clear on her pretty face. She knew what was happening. Knew that things were moving along faster than they'd planned. Knew her baby was coming whether Thaus was there or not. But she wasn't ready to give up hope that her mate would make it home in time. She also wasn't dumb enough to ignore what her body was telling her, no matter how much she wanted to.

"Fine. Maybe that's a good idea."

But as Ariel moved toward the couch, she rubbed at her back again. Laying her down wouldn't help her or the baby, so Michaela adjusted her plan. She spun a chair out from the kitchen table and pushed it into the living area.

"Here. Sit here, facing the back."

Ariel raised an eyebrow but did as Michaela asked, sagging as she straddled the wooden laths that made up the back support. "Oh, why does this feel so much better?"

Michaela placed her hands on Ariel's back and pushed, rubbing the soreness, using counterpressure to relieve the ache. "The baby needs to move a little. It's probably putting a little too much pressure on your coccyx."

Ariel snorted a laugh. "Only you would still call it a coccyx."

"Sorry. Tailbone." Michaela grinned and leaned forward, catching Ariel's eye. "Is that better, Doctor?"

"Much." Ariel moaned through another contraction, though this one seemed less intense. Less painful. Michaela rubbed her back through it all, her fingers dancing over the tightened muscles underneath them. The heels of her palms pressing deep until Ariel finally relaxed again. "It's time, isn't it?"

"You already know the answer to that."

Ariel nodded, her shoulders rolling forward. "I know. I was hoping for a miracle, though."

Her voice, the sadness there. The loneliness and fear. Michaela could practically feel those same emotions, could truly empathize with her friend's suffering. But she still needed to redirect Ariel's thoughts away from what was missing and toward what she was receiving.

"You're about to deliver a little miracle, Ariel," Michaela said. "Just not quite the way you'd hoped."

Ariel sighed, her hand going down to rest on top of her bump. "You're right. I know you're right."

"I'm always right, especially about babies. Speaking of which, it's time to check on the little one." Michaela slowly, deliberately slid her hands over Ariel's hips to her swollen belly. She closed her eyes and focused, truly concentrated on the little wolf shifter within. A solid heartbeat in a slightly off position, but nothing felt dangerous or possibly complicated. The little bugger was simply ready to come out. He or she was coming soon. Definitely soon.

"Everything okay?"

Michaela smiled as she met Ariel's worried eyes. "Everything is great. Position is a tiny bit off, but nothing too bad. That baby's just going to make you work a little harder to deal with the pain."

"Of course." Ariel rolled her eyes then rested her cheek on the back of her hands, serious once more. "He's going to miss the birth, isn't he?"

Michaela didn't need Ariel to say his name to know exactly whom she meant. "Probably. I'll be here with you every second, though. I know it's not the same, but you're not alone in this."

Ariel's eyes teared up and her face reddened. "I'm so glad I called you to help me."

"So am I. And not just because I met my mate here." Michaela helped Ariel to her feet then wrapped her arms around the shewolf's shoulders, giving her a hug from the side to accommodate the baby between them. "I want you to go lie down and rest. Stay off your back. In fact, lie on your side with a pillow between your knees. If the baby doesn't naturally move into position in the next few hours, we'll get more creative."

"Creative sounds painful."

Okay. Michaela could lie to her about one thing. "It probably won't be. Go on and rest now. You're going to meet your baby soon enough."

With a worried sort of smile, Ariel turned and headed down the hall, closing the bedroom door behind her with a soft snick. Michaela sagged into the corner of the couch, her heart heavy with worry for her friend. They needed to get her mate back. They needed to prepare. That baby was coming whether they were ready or not, and the men were all off hunting and fighting dark things. Not an ideal situation for any of them.

Michaela had just stood, thinking she'd make a pot of tea to ready herself for the long day ahead, when Phego, Colt, and a third man she didn't know raced through the front door. The three all wore simple, baggy cargo shorts, the kind Ariel kept on the porch for when one of the men shifted. The fact that they'd thrown those on instead of the clothes they'd left outside, the fact that they didn't take the time to go back to wherever they'd hidden those outfits, spoke more to her than anything.

Phego ran straight for her, his hands going to her shoulders the second he was close enough. His touch almost frenzied as he whispered, "Are you okay?"

Michaela smiled, examining him with every brush of her hands. "Of course. I'm not the one chasing beasts through the woods. Are you okay?"

"I'm fine. We lost the scent trail, though." His arm slipped around her, his warmth calling her in a way nothing else could. Michaela didn't have time to enjoy it, didn't have time to sink into his touch and relish that connection, though. She had a job to do.

"Ariel will be thrilled that her mate is back."

The man across the room frowned. "I'm not Thaus."

"This is another Dire," Phego said. "I called him for backup."

"When is Thaus coming back?" she asked, dreading the answer. She'd been so hopeful, so happy to see a third man.

"Couple of days yet," Deus said, the shifter watching her and Phego with interest. He dipped his head, keeping his eyes locked on hers. "I'm Deus, brother to Phego and Thaus. You smell like Phego there."

His words hung heavy with question, his meaning clear.

"I'm Michaela. Midwife for Ariel." In a moment of daring, she bumped her hip against Phego's and grinned. "I smell like my mate."

A muscle in Deus' forehead jumped, almost an unconscious tic. "I figured that part out."

Which meant Phego hadn't told him. The weight of that fact deadened something inside of her, made everything seem to dull. But there wasn't time to deal with hurt feelings and lacerated hearts. She had a job to do, one that didn't end at a specific time of day.

Michaela shook her head, pulling away from Phego so she could see his face. So she could make her point clear. "I don't know that Ariel will make it a couple of days. She's in labor."

"Shit," Phego growled. "What can we do?"

Deus shrugged, almost casual in a room filled with stress. "We call Luc."

"You want to bring Luc here? Around a pregnant woman?" Phego asked, sounding incredulous. Michaela didn't know who Luc was, but she had a feeling she didn't want to meet him. Not if the tone in Phego's voice was any indication of what kind of person Luc was.

"No," Deus said, pulling out a phone from the bag he'd brought inside with him. "The situation has changed from when we made the decision not to call him in. We need to adjust the mission. I want to send Luc to take over for the father. That way, the investigation into the explosives and threat to Blaze can continue, but Thaus is here for the birth of his child."

Phego nodded. "Do it. Call him."

Deus took off through the door, his fingers flying over the screen of his phone. Colt watched from his spot at the entrance to the kitchen, the one he'd been hovering in since he came inside.

"Where's he going?" Colt asked, looking wary. Angry, even.

"To make a phone call," Phego said, still with his hand on Michaela's arm. Refusing to break that connection. Something that played with her emotions in a way that wasn't fair. He touched her, but he didn't tell anyone about her. He had sex with her, but he didn't accept her as his mate.

Colt looked from one to the other—taking in their position, the way they were joined, and their body language. He frowned. "I'll walk with him to give you two a moment. Besides, no one should be left alone right now."

As soon as the other shifter stepped outside, Phego pulled Michaela back into his arms. She went willingly enough, needing that comfort, craving his touch. But she didn't hug him back.

Phego nuzzled into her neck and groaned as he pressed her against him. "Where's Ariel?"

"Lying down. You didn't tell your brother you'd found your mate?"

"There wasn't time. We were following a scent, one that's almost impossible to track. The damn thing just keeps ghosting... I don't know what's going on."

The candor, the open rawness of his voice, was new. As was the way he clung to her as if he needed her. As if he couldn't stand the thought of letting her go. This was her mate—the roughest, harshest man she'd ever met—shaken in a way that scared her.

"I don't either, but we'll figure it out," she said, rubbing her hands over his back, hoping the lie sounded true. "We have to."

Phego sighed, clenching his hands on her flesh almost to the point of pain before pulling away. "I should check with Deus."

Michaela nodded, letting him go. Watching him walk away. Colt came back inside a moment later, looking haggard and tired.

"Are you ready to go back to bed? There are still a few hours before sunrise."

Michaela nodded, definitely tired, knowing she should rest for Ariel. It would be a long day ahead of them, but she needed. She yearned. "Just give me a minute."

She waited for Colt to mount the stairs before heading for the porch. Phego stood there, arms braced against the railing, leaning forward with his head down. Looking exhausted and stressed and so very defeated. Michaela came up behind him, keeping her footsteps loud enough so as not to shock him. Running her hand along his bare back once she reached him.

She pressed a soft kiss to his spine as he shivered beneath her touch. "I'm heading back to bed."

Phego turned, pulling her into his arms and running his nose along the length of hers. "I wish I were coming with you."

Michaela sagged into his arms, wrapping hers around his neck. "I wish you were too."

They stood wrapped around one another for a long time, seconds turning into minutes. The woods were still so silent, so dark. It was as if they were in their own world. At least, until Deus came pounding up the stairs.

"Our leader is an asshole." He gave a quick head nod to Michaela, not even glancing twice at the way she and Phego were snuggled close. "When he finally picked up, all he said was, 'It's in motion.' As if that means something."

"What it is he talking about?" Phego asked, still clinging to Michaela. She didn't mind a bit, nor did she pull away. Not yet.

"Who the fuck knows?" Deus blanched and shot Michaela a shallow smile. "Sorry for the language."

"I've heard and said fuck before," she said, shrugging. "I'm sure I'll do it again."

Deus raised his eyebrows and looked to Phego. "She's

cool. Keep her. I'll get a tracking phone in her hands as soon as we're done here."

Phego growled, pulling her tighter and nuzzling back into her neck. Ignoring his packmate. "Go to bed. Get some rest. It's going to be a long day."

Michaela nodded into his chest, still clutching him. Still needing his touch. Still worried about where they were in their mating even though Deus' words and Phego's closeness had soothed the worst of her fears. "When this is done, when the baby is born, will you and I—"

"One thing at a time, little mate." Phego pulled back, arms still on her shoulders, ducking to look her square in the eye even as her heart jumped at his use of the word mate. "Let's get through the next couple of days, the baby coming, and the threat in the woods. Then we'll talk. I promise."

Michaela nodded. "I'll hold you to that."

Phego gave her a quick kiss, barely more than a brush of his lips against hers before he let her go. "I'm learning how. It's hard, but I'm trying."

Her smile was unavoidable. "That's all I can ask for."

"Oh, no," he said as he headed down the steps leading off the porch. "You can ask for more. I'm an asshole and a bit stunted in this area, but you can ask me for anything. Everything. I have a feeling I'd give it to you."

And then he was gone.

Fifteen

Phego woke with a start, a sense of dread yanking him from his nap in a harsh blow to his being. He recognized that feeling, had battled its cold clutch around his heart more than once in his life. The time his brother had come to call for him, to bring him home. The time Mammon had sent him and Levi to crawl into an old, abandoned mine with unsteady walls. The time Bez had gone off to fight a vampire clan alone. All moments of tragedy barely averted, of battles impossible to win falling on his pack's side in a twist of fate that always brought them closer together. Death was coming. The specter had infiltrated the woods, standing close and ready, hungry for the souls long denied him. Someone would be fighting for their life today, and he could only hope it wasn't Ariel or the baby.

Or Michaela…

He jumped out of his makeshift bed in the hallway at the thought of his mate and padded out into the living room. Deus was already up, staring at computer screens just as Phego expected. The shifter would never shirk his guard duty responsibility, but he would definitely use the time to his advantage. Multitasking was an understatement for what Deus could do.

The shifter barely even glanced up as his fingers flew over the keyboard. "Luc is already on mission site as far as I can tell. How that creepy psychic knew we needed him before we called, I have no clue. I really should stop questioning him, though."

"You think he'll send Thaus back here?"

Deus raised an eyebrow and glanced at the entrance to the kitchen before whispering, "I think he already did. Thaus' GPS ping is moving closer."

Phego nodded, cautiously optimistic. If Thaus made it back, they'd have another Dire to fight with. Three against one—no matter how big that one was—were far better odds. He just needed to have patience and hope the man made it in time.

For more than just the coming hunt.

Ariel shuffled out of the kitchen looking positively haggard and exhausted. And bigger. How her stomach could have grown in the few hours they'd all been resting, he had no idea. But it had. She seemed almost ready to topple over at the weight of it pulling her forward. Michaela followed the pregnant shewolf, a hand on Ariel's back. A concerned expression on her beautiful face.

"C'mere, sis," Deus called, holding up a hand for Ariel. She trudged across the room, settling in beside Deus in a move Phego hadn't expected. Deus wasn't exactly known for his social skills, and Ariel was usually too uncomfortable around new people to interact with them. Though he guessed Deus wasn't really new. They'd met...once.

"What are you doing?" Ariel asked as Deus typed away one-handed.

"I wrote up a quick algorithm to concoct names from the letters in yours and Thaus'. I mean, I had to use his whole name of Sathanus to get more options, but it's cool. It's a badass name. The system then eliminated any options that were too hard to pronounce based on the phonetics of the romance language roots. We should have some stellar options here in a minute."

Ariel sighed and closed her eyes, holding her belly as if trying to support the weight. "You are not naming my child."

"You have to hear me out on this one…"

But Deus' words were lost as Phego's mate brushed up against his side. Her warm, welcoming scent enveloped him, calmed him, spoke to him on some primal level. He itched to hold her, to wrap her in his arms and take comfort from her flesh against his, but he couldn't. If he did, he'd be lost to her, and it wasn't the time. Not yet.

Soon.

Still, he gave her a lean and a growl to let her know he liked her closeness. "Something you wanted, Doc?"

She grinned, humming. "Yes, but that's not really possible right now." She grinned up at him as he groaned and moved closer. "When will Thaus get here?"

Phego leaned down, letting his lips touch the soft skin in front of her ear as he whispered to her. "No idea, but he's moving this way."

Michaela rubbed her cheek against his, a subtle sort of move that had his beast howling for her and his cock hardening. "She won't make it more than a few hours, if I had to guess."

Phego pulled back a step and nodded, seeing the same signs she did. Needing to keep his mind clear and focused on the important issues they were going to have to face. Knowing they were in a race to the end.

Before he could move too far away, Michaela slid her

fingers between his, grabbing hold of his hand as if for added support. Phego had never held hands with another person before. Had never felt the comfort of another's touch in that way. He stared down at where their hands were joined, brown and white stripes woven together to make a picture of them as one. He liked that. Liked the connection to her. Liked the feel of her skin against his. She was winning him over, her quiet patience and easy smile something he couldn't ignore.

"I have my own cabin," he said, words tumbling from his mouth, his brain unable to keep up as his mate gave him a confused sort of smile. "This is where Thaus and Ariel live. Mine is…farther out."

"I had no idea," Michaela said. She licked her bottom lip, fascinating him with that little flash of pink. "Maybe you could show me—"

"Michaela." Colt appeared at the front door, his eyes finding Michaela. Something in his stance caught Phego's attention, made him pull his mate in closer. Made him have to fight the urge to protect her. Colt must have noticed the move because he stayed on the opposite side of the screen door, not coming into the cabin at all.

"Hey, Phego. Morning," Colt said. An unusual greeting for him. Colt's eyes darted to Ariel, taking in the sight of her leaning against Deus' shoulder. She looked to be napping again; the exhaustion from earlier still evidenced by the way her lips turned down. Perhaps that was it—Colt had reservations about being near Ariel. He'd probably never been involved with a woman giving birth before. At least, it didn't seem as if he had, judging from the anxious air around him. An air Michaela didn't appear to recognize.

"Morning, Colt," she said. Still holding Phego's hand. Still connected to him. Phego made no move to let her go, either.

"I need to speak to you. Outside." He shot a pointed look to Phego. "Alone."

Michaela sighed, glancing up in a way that screamed apology. "I'll be right back."

Phego squeezed her hand once then let her go, knowing he'd have her in his arms again in a few minutes. Certain of it. He watched her walk outside, stared at the way her hips swung under her skirt, catching Deus' furrowed brow and worried stare once the door shut.

"What?" Phego asked.

Deus shrugged. "Odd relationship, that's all."

"He's her bodyguard, and she's an Omega," Ariel said, sounding irritated. Obviously not napping as Phego had assumed. "You can't blame her Alpha for sending someone to watch over her."

Deus sat deeper into the couch, crossing his ankle over his knee and looking down at Ariel in that inquisitive way he had. "I don't blame the Alpha for sending a bodyguard. But I do wonder what the bodyguard's going to be doing once the baby comes."

They both turned to look at Phego, Deus' meaning clear. Once the baby came and Michaela was technically no longer needed… What then? Would she stay? Would they all leave together? Would she go back to her pack with Colt?

Phego didn't have an answer. "We'll get to that when we get to that."

Deus laughed and dropped his head back, looking as if he was a cat about to catch a canary. "She's really got your number, doesn't she? You are such a—"

But the sound of growling and snapping drew all their attention before Deus could finish his sentence. The room went silent and still, every person focused on the noise from outside.

A second later, they exploded into organized chaos.

Ariel jumped up from where she'd been lounging on the couch and took two steps toward the door, but her body betrayed her. A sudden burst of liquid spread down her legs, and she almost doubled over in pain, both hands going to her round belly.

"Oh, hell," she said, groaning out the last word.

Deus was up without pause, hurrying toward her. Phego beat him there, though. Grabbing her arm and turning her toward the stairs as his brain focused on one thing. One threat. One need to protect beyond the woman he was bound to.

Michaela.

"Up." He led her to the hallway, not letting go until she had a hold of the handrail and started to move. "Get up there and stay put. We'll come for you when we know everything's okay."

Deus appeared at his side and tossed a black bag up to the top landing. A mission bag. One that was probably filled with guns, ammunition, knives, and explosives.

"Good call," Phego said as he turned toward the door. He had his mate to worry about.

"Ain't my first time." Deus said just as an attic door clicked closed. Ariel was safe; it was time to fight. Deus must have felt the same because he was on Phego's heels in a split second. The two raced outside just as a scream ripped through the air. One from outside. One from Michaela. Phego's heart crashed in his chest as his feet hit the rough wooden planks of the porch, seeking her out, ready to defend her in every way he could. Deus matched Phego growl for growl, step for step, looking ready to fight anything in their path as they crossed the porch.

Neither of them made it to the steps.

In the morning glow of the sun rising over the treetops around them, a violent scene played out like something from a nightmare. A wolf—bigger than any Dire Phego had ever seen other than himself—stood at the edge of the tree line.

Stood was the wrong word, though. The wolf hunched and jumped, shaking something. Tearing it apart as—

A body. The wolf had a body between his jaws, shaking it like a rag doll. The body flopped with every jerk, blood dripping and spraying all over the grass. That person was obviously dead, though too badly damaged to recognize. A fact that sent Phego's stomach to his feet and the name Michaela screaming through his mind.

The animal stopped when he noticed the two Dires on the porch, practically grinning at them from across the grass. And then he spat out his prey. His pale-skinned prey.

Colt.

But Phego couldn't be bothered with a dead guard. Not when the beast standing before him was something straight out of the hell of his past. The spots along the animal's neck and back were clearly defined, the pattern obvious, the wolf familiar. Too familiar. But there was no way. After centuries upon centuries, it was not possible that Phego could be seeing that particular nightmare come to life. But he was. As was Deus, whose sharp intake of breath told Phego his assumption was right. That wolf, that Dire, was no stranger to them. Even though he wasn't pack. At least, not any longer.

But the worst, beyond the ghost from his past and the dead bodyguard, came when the beast moved closer. When he revealed his final secret.

Michaela.

Phego's mate—his gorgeous, sexy, kind-hearted mate— stood beside the wolf at the edge of the woods. Still as a stone with no expression on her face. Doing nothing as the creature murdered her packmate and bodyguard. As Phego's heart hardened over and the dark voice inside his mind jeered that he'd been duped. That he'd been sold out. That...

Why wasn't she moving?

Sixteen

*M*ichaela walked outside after Colt with a bit of a spring in her step. Her mate had reached for her, smiled at her. Held her hand. Something so simple and sweet shouldn't have set her heart to thumping the way it had, but the man in question was Phego. Her reserved, stoic, often silent mate. Every single step, every little move of acceptance and affection, was something to be celebrated, it seemed.

But Ariel's baby was coming soon. Probably within the next day or two at most. Once the tiny bundle arrived, Michaela's job at the little cabin in the woods would be finished. She would no longer be needed. Would Phego still *want* her to stay? Would he demand she leave her pack to join him in his quiet existence? Would he even consider following her back to her pack? Not that she'd demand such a thing. While she loved her pack and her family there, Phego was her mate. He was her future. She'd do whatever she needed to that would work for the two of them as a unit. She could compromise. The question was, could he?

He'd told her about his cabin. Even seemed as if he wanted her to see it. So…maybe? Maybe to everything, but maybe was far better than no.

Michaela was too far into her thoughts to see what was wrong until she practically stumbled over it. Too focused on the future to see the threat right in front of her. At least, until it was too late.

"Don't be afraid," Colt said, yanking her back to attention. He stood ten yards away, almost to the tree line, with a large, spotted wolf at his side. A Dire Wolf.

"Is this Thaus? We should tell Phego he's here." Michaela let her voice fade, her words growing quieter as a chill of apprehension made her take a step back. Something in the animal's eyes felt off. Something about the way he took her in set her survival instincts on fire. Danger…he was pure and utter danger.

Colt shook his head, a slow and deliberate move she'd never seen him make. One that mimicked the heavy head of the wolf beside him. That was the moment she got it, that she knew. Something was wrong. Something was very, very wrong.

"What's happening here?" she asked, swallowing hard and planting her feet wide in case she needed to defend herself.

Colt didn't answer, just scowled and stood straight and tall as if unable to move. As if controlled. Michaela took another step back, ready to run, but the wolf's low growl stopped her in her tracks.

"Don't move. You'll be safe," Colt said, his voice stressed and quiet. His muscles tight. Definitely under some sort of sick Alpha order. "He just wants Phego."

The words were on her lips before her brain could think them through. "Well, he can't have him."

Colt groaned, his head falling back, his muscles trembling as they locked into some sort of hyperextension.

He looked as if he was being torn in two, as if he could be ripped into pieces at any second. But even Colt's twisted position couldn't hide the destruction happening beside him. The wolf shifted human, the man appearing almost from within the fur in an uneven roll that spoke to something being broken between the two forms. Bones and ligaments tearing through flesh only to be reabsorbed, blood falling to the forest floor as skin and fur split over and over again. The sounds, the sights, the smells…all of it worked together to make her sick stomach roil. She swallowed hard, fighting back the urge to expel her breakfast.

The man who emerged from within the fur of the wolf didn't seem fazed, though. Tall and thick, he exuded a type of malice she'd never been forced to endure before. Reeked of evil and age and wrong. But his eyes—those light gray eyes—were the final straw. She bent at the waist, losing her stomach across the grass. Unable not to see those eyes. She recognized them. Saw much more of her mate in the man before her than she cared to admit.

"Who are you?" she asked as she wiped her mouth, already knowing the answer. Or at least, the direction it would take.

"What? You don't see the family resemblance?" He turned his lips up in some sort of bastardization of a smile, half-rotted teeth dark against the paleness of his mouth. Leering at her from under his heavy brow. "The fates gave you to my family when they tied you to Belphegor, whom you know as Phego. That means they gave you to me. Why don't you come and give me a hug, sis?"

Phego. This man was related to Phego. This evil was in their lineage, this perversion of nature related to her mate. She fought not to be sick again.

When Michaela didn't move, the man shrugged. Feigning disinterest, even as he stalked closer. "No affection for me? Phego's only kin? That's hurtful, sister mine. You deserve to be punished for that sort of disobedience."

The way he spat punished, the way his eyes practically glittered with a want she didn't have the wherewithal to think about, chilled Michaela to the bone. She needed to go. Needed to run. She needed to find Phego. He would know what to do with…this.

"What do you want?" Michaela asked, taking another step backward, looking for any sign of escape.

The man laughed, his husky chuckle terrifying. "What I've always wanted, but we'll get to that later. How about I take care of our little eavesdropper first?"

Before she could respond, the man before her shifted wolf once more. This time, there was no pause, no slow roll. It was as if he was meant to be wolf, his human form simply enveloped into the fur of his beast. The shift human was the one that was broken. From human to beast appeared easier, more natural. More instinctual.

Within the blink of an eye, he'd changed forms…

And attacked.

"Colt," she yelled as the wolf clamped his teeth around the man's waist. The wolf roared and twisted, throwing Colt to the ground with an almost lazy-looking move. Too big, too strong. Especially for her. As the beast tore into Colt's flesh, as the blood began to spray and the man hollered in pain, Michaela screamed. The wolf had her bodyguard pinned beneath him. There was nothing she could do, nothing to stop the wolf as he attacked his prey. It was all over too fast. One bite, one snap of jaws, one sharp head twist, and she knew…Colt was dead.

She screamed again.

The beast snarled and kept attacking anyway, tossing Colt's body about like a piece of garbage. Making more noise than she'd thought possible. And Michaela…well, she couldn't look away. She couldn't excuse herself from witnessing the horror. This was somehow her fault, and she owed Colt more than to run off and hide. She would look for every opportunity to save the remains of her friend from his murderer. She would do…something. As soon as her body started answering her brain again.

Before she could decide what, the door of the cabin flew open, and Phego rushed outside with Deus right behind him. Michaela wanted to run to her mate, wanted to feel his arms around her and know she was safe, but as the wolf dragged Colt's lifeless body closer to the porch, she saw Phego's face. The pain, the shuttering of every possible emotion. Something about the scene sent him running, at least mentally. Something betrayed his trust. But what? She hadn't set this up. In fact, she felt more in danger at that moment than ever before. So why was her mate looking at her as if she'd betrayed him? And why couldn't she get her feet to move like she wanted them to?

The wolf stopped growling and stood still when he seemed to notice his witnesses, dropping Colt's body to the ground as if it were nothing. As if it weren't a person.

"Gressil," Phego yelled, his voice sharp and direct. Confirming her fears—they knew each other. They were likely family as the wolf, Gressil, had implied. A tear burned a path down her cheek, and she couldn't stop shaking. This was bad. This was all bad. Had Phego somehow set them up? Were Ariel and the baby in danger?

The wolf shifted human again, stepping right beside Michaela as he did. She stiffened, unable not to. Unable to move a muscle as the simple power of his form grew close to her. Unable to move…at all.

Shit, even if she'd wanted to, she literally couldn't get her body to respond to her thoughts. She was trapped, frozen. Completely under Gressil's control.

"So you do remember me," Gressil said in a mocking sort of tone. He reached out and dragged a finger down Michaela's arm, making her shiver. Making her want to vomit once more.

Phego's jaw ticked once, twice. A tell of his frustration. A sure sign of a burning rage within him. Rage at who or what, though, she couldn't be sure. "Sort of hard to forget the man who led me to my death."

"Oh, little brother. Are you still mad about that?" Gressil chuckled. "I would have figured a millennium or two would have chilled out that bad attitude."

Phego didn't take the bait of that statement. "You should be dead."

"No, you should be." Gressil snapped and snarled, his canines descending and his wolf fur sprouting. Losing most of his control to the beast within. "You're the fallen son, the failure to the line. I did what I was told. I lived up to every expectation our Alpha set, while you ran about trying to please our parents as if they mattered in the grand scheme of the pack."

"That was no pack," Deus said, his voice rough with his growl.

Gressil lurched closer to the porch, his hand clamping around Michaela's wrist to keep her next to him. "That pack was everything. I killed my own parents to show my loyalty to the Alpha, but no. My bastard brother, the one the Alpha truly wanted dead, disappeared before I could finish my assignment. I couldn't prove I'd done all that he wanted, so I was thrown out."

"What are you doing here?" Phego asked with no emotion to his voice. No expression on his face. Stoic once more. Closed off. Lost to her.

Michaela stumbled as Gressil yanked her forward, the control over her muscles loosening enough that she could move. Not run, not escape, not have full functionality of her body…but she could *move*. Which was so much better than the feeling of being frozen in place that she'd been fighting.

"I've been looking for you, brother." Gressil spat the last word as if the syllable was something foul. Something dirty and wrong. "It was a nice little plot twist that I found you with a mate by your side."

Phego didn't flinch, didn't even look her way. He seemed disconnected from her in every way, which killed Michaela inside. More tears fell as Gressil's claws punctured her arm, the pain searing. Blood dripped as well, the soft pats of each drop falling adding to the nightmare playing out in her mind. Why wouldn't Phego help her?

"Let her go," Deus said, looking ready to attack even as Phego simply stared.

"No, I don't think I will." Gressil grinned. "I saw you two in the barn the other day, Belphegor. Very hot. Think I might just take her as a prize."

Michaela couldn't help it. She cried and tried to pull away from the disgusting creature, gasping a small yelp as his claws dug deeper. Phego finally looked her way, finally caught her eye. Finally broke. One second, that was all it took. His face cleared, his worry shining through, and the warmth of his attention held her in its grasp.

An act. It had to be an act. He would help her. He would save her.

"Release her," Phego said. "This is our fight. She has nothing to do with it."

"I disagree, brother. She has a lot to do with it. Or at least, she could." He ran a finger along Michaela's face, his claw skimming her cheek. His smell making her gag. "I wonder how much she'd scream if I skinned her alive. How much would you, Belphegor, if I made you watch?"

Phego's eyes went from light gray to pure, chrome-like

silver in a blink, his wolf making itself known. "Won't happen."

"No? Then how about I just kill you instead?" Gressil shifted again, his speed still something impressive to behold. But Michaela had seen this change already, had memorized his moves. Like a baseball player eyeing the first pitch as it whizzed through the strike zone, she'd watched and learned and set up some sort of timing in her mind. She knew his tells. And as he shifted, she felt her body come back under her control. She had one shot. One chance to try not to die.

And she was going to take it.

Before Gressil could take one step toward her mate, before he was fully wolf, even, Michaela was on him. Her human arms stretched around his neck as much as she could make them, and she laid her body out across his spine to unbalance him. She pressed her feet under his hips and clamped on with her knees, riding him. Unable to stop him, but using simple physics to slow him down.

Gressil twisted and turned, snapping at her, but she refused to let go. Refused to simply let him kill her mate. Not if she could stop it.

"Michaela, no!"

She didn't know who yelled her name, didn't see what was happening on the porch. She closed her eyes and held on as the wolf bucked and snarled. As he backed into the forest. As he twisted and snarled and fought.

As he reared up on his back legs.

As he surrendered to gravity and fell back.

As he crushed her into something hard and unforgiving.

Seventeen

From where Phego stood, Michaela looked terrified. He doubted the rest of the group could see how much, though. Deus didn't know her yet, and Gressil—fuck, Gressil. If Phego weren't so worried about his mate, he might just drag this confrontation out so he could figure out how the fuck his brother, who should have been dead, was there. Phego had been the information gatherer for their group for years, had learned and mastered ways of torture that always loosened lips. He wanted to know how the fucker had survived the pack extermination, how he'd lived for so long under the radar, and if there were any more Dires like him out there.

Yes, the work side of his brain wanted to break out knives and pliers and torches to get his information. The human side of him wanted answers. The wolf side just wanted his mate safe and away from the sick fuck his brother had obviously become.

He may have doubted Michaela for a split second, but

not after he saw her face. Not after he recognized the feel of an Alpha order hanging over her. Not after her eyes filled with tears as she watched him. He needed her, cared for her, and wanted her safe. He also trusted her enough to know she had nothing to do with the shitshow she seemed to be in the middle of.

"Release her," Phego said, curling a lip at his brother in a subtle challenge. "This is our fight. She has nothing to do with it."

But Gressil never did take well to challenges, and he continued that streak. "I disagree, brother. She has a lot to do with it. Or at least, she could." With a cocky smirk that sent ice racing along Phego's spine and made his inner wolf snarl, Gressil ran a finger along Michaela's face, his claw pressing into her cheek. "I wonder how much she'd scream if I skinned her alive. How much would you, Belphegor, if I made you watch?"

Claws out, eyes tightening into their wolf vision, he was ready. "Won't happen."

"No? Then how about I just kill you instead?"

"Stay with Ariel," Phego said to Deus as he exploded into motion. He didn't need to wait for Deus to respond. His brother would keep the Omega safe. Hell, the second Michaela got away from Gressil, Deus would keep her safe, too. Phego didn't even have to ask. But saving Michaela was Phego's primary plan, his only goal. Separate his mate from the danger, then eliminate the threat.

Phego jumped from the porch and dove straight for Gressil, shifting in midair. He landed with his teeth bared, his claws out, and his wolf ready to tear into his brother's flesh. But Gressil was no weakling, no untrained wolf.

And apparently, Michaela had plans of her own.

She jumped on top of Gressil, wrapping her body around him like a cowboy on a bucking bronc. Holding on to his neck in a way that Phego was almost proud of. But that didn't last for long. Gressil wasn't one not to fight back. He roared and jumped, trying to knock her off his back. Before Phego could get to them, Gressil reared up and fell back, slamming Michaela between his body and a tree.

She fell off and lay limp in the grass, unconscious. Unprotected.

He hated to leave her like that, but Phego saw his chance and he had to take it. He rushed Gressil, knocking him down with a vicious hit to the side. Gressil wasn't an easy opponent, though. He jumped up and came storming toward Phego, slamming into him with teeth bared. Phego fell back, taking Gressil with him, narrowly avoiding teeth and claws as he tried to gain the upper hand. Or paw, as it were.

Phego fought hard, using his body weight to force the fight away from his mate. He couldn't see Michaela, couldn't focus on her for a second, but he could try to get Gressil out of her vicinity so Deus could take care of her. That was his goal—as least, his first one. After she was safe, he could figure out what to do about his brother. Information retrieval and death, or just immediate death…there wasn't another option for him. Gressil wasn't walking out of the forest.

It took Phego a few tries, but eventually, he managed to get his claws deep into his brother's hide. Gressil yelped and fell back, limping away. Phego followed him, head down, hackles up, snarling. Ready to fight. Ready to kill. But Gressil wasn't ready to die, apparently. He shifted to his human form, the move one that wasn't as smooth or as easy as it should have been. A sure sign he'd been in his wolf form for far too long.

"Good hit, brother," Gressil said, grabbing his neck as if trying to hold in the blood pouring down his chest. He shot a glance around the clearing as if looking for an escape, but Phego didn't give him one. Wouldn't. He just kept backing

Gressil up toward the barn, toward the place he'd use if he decided to go for information retrieval. Away from Michaela…and Ariel.

"What, you won't talk to me?" Gressil laughed, the sound pained and wrong. That throat wound looked deadly, which meant Phego needed to move faster. Make a decision. But Gressil didn't seem to know how to hold his tongue. "You always were a self-righteous little bastard."

Phego took the bait that time, shifting human. Staying close to his prey as he herded him back. "I am no bastard."

"No, you're not. You were the prized son. The youngest, yet the one groomed to be Alpha."

"Not true."

"That," Gressil yelled, pointing, his eyes wide and burning bright with some sort of fanatical fire. "You never even saw it. The Alpha wanted you to replace him when the time came, so they were grooming you. Making sure you were ready for the challenges, while I was forced to go out and find my own training."

"Are you jealous? Do you not remember that last day? Our parents tried to have me killed."

Gressil laughed as he edged around the clearing at the back of the cabin, the sound sending chills up Phego's spine. "Our parents didn't try to kill you. That was all me. You were the perfect Alpha son, ready to be promoted into pack leadership. Handed that position on a silver fucking platter. But I wanted that spot. I deserved it."

Gressil lunged, rushing past Phego in an effort to head toward the cabin. He was fast, too, but Phego was faster. Phego had always been faster. He stepped in Gressil's way and braced himself, a wall of muscle and human that Gressil had no chance at forcing his way through.

As Gressil hit, Phego twisted and struck with his claws, taking another handful of flesh from the man just to prove he could. Gressil bounced back, falling over, grunting and grabbing his torn open bicep.

"Fuck, what the hell are you?" Gressil asked, spitting his words.

But Phego was running out of patience. He stepped over the fallen Dire, one foot on his shoulder, his weight holding Gressil down. "Where have you been?"

"Fuck you," Gressil spat, writhing in an attempt to push off his captor. The blood flowing from his neck had slowed, whether from too much loss or healing, Phego didn't know. Didn't care, either. He had information to get, and that meant making sure Gressil knew death was coming, but keeping him hopeful enough that he'd be spared to flap his lips.

That meant getting a little rough.

Phego wasn't new to the tactic; he'd mastered it centuries ago. He slid his foot over Gressil's blood-covered chest, heading toward his throat. Pressing on Gressil's neck with his heel. Death then hope. Phego pressed down, cutting off his brother's air supply for a few seconds before releasing the pressure to allow Gressil to breathe. He did it again. And again. Repeating the move, stretching the time his brother couldn't breathe for longer and longer until Gressil lay still, silent, and defeated.

"Let's try this again," Phego said as he leaned over and pressed his toes against Gressil's chin. "Where have you been?"

This time, Gressil didn't hesitate. "Running packs down in Australia."

"Why Australia?"

"It's easy to hide out there. Especially for us Dires."

Phego kept his calm on the outside, but inside, his mind spun hard with that new piece of information. "There are more?"

Gressil chuckled and spat a glob of blood onto the

grass. "What? You thought you were special? You and your so-called pack?"

Phego took one second too long to respond, a single moment of shock overtaking him and slowing his reaction. But that was enough. Gressil grabbed his ankle and twisted, throwing him off as the injured Dire jumped to his feet. The two shifted wolf once more, Gressil just a hair faster than Phego.

But again, that was all it took.

Gressil had Phego pinned in a split second, had his teeth on Phego's neck in the same moment. There was no time to react, no time to fight back. There was nothing left...

Which was why seeing a branch come out of nowhere and smack his brother upside the head shook Phego to his very core. Gressil rolled off him, grunting as he fell to the side. Phego jumped to his feet, ready to war, ready to battle, but instead, he froze. Seeing Michaela standing on the other side of Gressil's body, branch in hand and looking like some sort of Amazon princess ready to fight to the death stole his breath. How could she be so strong? How could she be so loyal as to risk her life for him already?

And how the hell had he gotten so lucky as to have her by his side?

But those thoughts all needed to wait. Phego pounced toward her, ready to shove her back toward the house and safety, but it was too late. Gressil had recovered his feet and was already bearing down on her. Phego forced himself to move faster, determined, ready to jump between them. Gressil reached her first, rearing up on his back legs. Mouth open and teeth bared as he came down at her. Phego pushed himself more, desperate to get to her. To save her. Hoping that branch she was holding up as a shield could give him the extra second or two he needed to—

The sound of a single gunshot exploded through the clearing.

Gressil and Michaela fell, both bloodied. Both hit. Phego's heart nearly stopped, but his feet didn't. He turned for Michaela, needing to check on his mate, to make sure she was okay. To save her. Deus cut him off.

"Finish this," he yelled, dragging Michaela away from where Gressil still lay in the grass. Phego put his faith in his brother, his Dire brother, and twisted around to finish off Gressil. Fuck the information he might have. If there were other Dires, so be it. His pack would find them. But first…

Gressil rolled, his flesh still hanging open along his throat, his fur stained red along one side of his chest. The same color red as Michaela's blood…the blood she spilled because of him. While Gressil may not have been the one to directly injure his mate, it was still his fault. And Phego would make him pay.

With one snarl and a dive, Phego's wolf pinned Gressil to the ground by his neck and bit down deep. The injured wolf yelped and pulled, trying to escape, flailing his legs to gain purchase on anything he could, but Phego was focused. Ready. Pissed the fuck off. Gressil had caused his mate to be hurt. He'd put her in danger.

Gressil would die for those sins.

And die he did.

With his teeth buried in Gressil's throat, Phego curled his claws under his flesh. Tearing. Pulling. Ending.

Phego stared into Gressil's silver eyes—the ones so much like his own that it sent a rock plummeting into his gut—as they went dark and lifeless. Still, he held his brother down, refusing to let go. Unable to give up. There was so much he wanted to know, so much information he should have collected, but Gressil was a threat to his mate. An enemy to his very future. One that needed to be destroyed for Phego even to think about moving forward in his life. One he himself had to dispatch if he was ever going to believe the past wasn't coming back to haunt him. And though killing his own brother felt wrong in a lot of ways, it also rebalanced the scales in his mind. Gressil had tried to have him killed, had murdered his own parents. What Phego was doing was payback.

When Gressil finally lay dead, bloodless and still on the forest floor, Phego released him. Released the weight of something that had long hung around his own neck, too. Fuck information, fuck history, and fuck his brother for manipulating him into thinking his own parents had tried to have him killed. Gressil's death brought him no sadness or sense of loss—it only brought relief.

And exhaustion.

Phego's every muscle burned, his bones aching as fought to catch his breath. He fell backward, shifting in mid-roll. Ending up naked on his knees with blood staining his chest and his claws still out. Still sharp. Still ready to attack. An animal in human form, so much like his brother.

"Here." Michaela appeared at his side and wrapped one of the blankets from the porch swing around his shoulders. Her kindness, her trust, reset something in Phego's brain. He wasn't like his brother—not really. Hell, not at all. He was honest and loyal, wary of strangers but never manipulative. He had a human side, one that had been locked up tight for too many years to count. One that his mate had finally helped him find.

Phego grabbed Michaela's hand, unable not to touch. Desperate to feel something other than fear or hate. She gripped him back just as hard, stepping in front of him and pulling his head against her stomach. Her fingers in his hair were a balm, a gift, a chance to soothe something that felt utterly broken.

"They shot you," he grumbled, sliding his hands up her back. Seeking any damage.

"Barely. Not even really a flesh wound. I'll be fine." She held him tight, supporting. Rubbing. Calming. Never letting him go. Never letting him forget that she was there for him. He wished he would have been there for her.

"I'm so sorry I didn't trust you," Phego said, his voice hoarse.

"It's okay." She pulled him tighter, letting him bury his face in her body. Giving of herself to comfort him. "We'll get there eventually."

Phego clutched her hips and kissed the curve of her stomach, unable to resist. Needing a piece of her like he needed air. "We will. I promise you, we will. No trying, only succeeding at being a mated couple. If you'll have me, because the fates know I don't deserve you."

Michaela gasped, her soft catch of breath matching the jerk of her fingers against his head. "We'll work this through together."

Even though she hadn't fully answered him, hadn't told him if she'd be his forever, Phego could only smile and nuzzle more of her body. He craved her, was desperate to have her naked and wrapped around him. Not for sex, though that was also on his mind. But no, he needed her comfort. Her calm. Her very presence.

"Together."

"Told you the armory would come in handy," Ariel said, breaking the soft intimacy of the moment.

"Shouldn't you be having a baby?" Phego asked, clinging to Michaela. Unable to resist peeking toward where Ariel and Deus stood together. "Thought you were in labor?"

"I *am* in labor, you jackass."

Michaela chuckled, still holding Phego against her with her hands in his hair. Still comforting him like no one else could. "That was a great shot."

Deus cackled. "Great shot? She clipped you."

"Sorry," Ariel said with a shrug, looking a little paler than normal. "I had a contraction as I fired. It knocked me off a bit."

Phego climbed to his feet, hanging on to Michaela as he did. "There are more Dires."

Deus grew serious. "We know. We heard. There's nothing we can do right at this moment, though."

"Is there a plan?" Ariel asked, rubbing her belly and frowning.

"Yes," Michaela said. She kissed Phego's cheek before walking away from him, making his wolf whine. He wasn't ready to let her out of his sight just yet. She must have understood because she shot a wink over her shoulder as she continued to walk away. "Let's all head inside. Ariel and I have a baby to deliver, and you two can contact whomever you need to contact to do whatever it is you're going to do."

"You sound so professional," Deus said, sounding sarcastic as all hell.

His mate wasn't one to back down from a challenge, though. "I can talk about placental abruptions and hemangiomas instead if you'd like."

"I'm good." Deus backed up, hands in the air.

But Phego wasn't ready for any of their laughing and joking. Nor was he ready for Michaela to walk away from him. He couldn't gain control of his wolf, not wholly. Couldn't stop his body from trembling.

"Mate," he croaked. Michaela stopped and spun, frowning, staring at him as if he'd grown a third head, so he tried again. "You're my mate."

She stared at him, her eyes worried. Her head cocked to one side. "Yes, I am."

"I want you to be," he murmured, trying to make her understand. Failing, though. Her frown deepened, and he growled his frustration. "I want you to be my mate. Forever."

She took a step closer. Just one. "You'll have to trust me. Completely."

He matched her step then doubled down, taking two more in quick succession. "I will. I do."

"You do?" Another step closer. Close enough to touch. To feel. To scent. Phego gave her question the attention it deserved, diving deep into his feelings and instincts. He *did* trust Michaela. Full trust, not some semblance of pieced-together loyalty, either.

"Yes." He grabbed her hand, pulling her against him. Wrapping his arms around her hips and yanking her almost off her feet. He couldn't help it. He needed her. "I was an idiot. A stupid, selfish idiot and I definitely don't deserve you. But I want you. I need you in my life."

Thankfully, Michaela didn't seem to mind him laying out his bad points. In fact, her face lit up, and a slow, sexy grin curled those pink lips he desired to taste again upward. "So you're going to keep me all to yourself, then?"

His answer was bold, direct, and to the point. And one hundred percent truthful. "Yes."

"You're going to take care of me?"

"I will. I promise."

"Us, too," Deus yelled. "Our pack will take care of you."

Phego shot him a glare, growling softly before refocusing on what was important. What mattered in that moment. On Michaela.

"They will take care of you. My brothers are protective," Phego said, leaning closer, licking a path up her neck to her ear before whispering, "But not in the same way that I'll take care of you, my mate."

"Yes," she hissed as he bit her earlobe.

Phego swallowed hard, fighting back his own demons one last time to spread himself at her feet. At her mercy. "Is that a yes to me taking care of you, or a yes to us being mates forever?"

She pulled back, her dark eyes twinkling. "Can't I have both?"

"Absolutely." Phego pressed his lips to hers, claiming her mouth with the smooth slide of his tongue. His mate. His. Always. It'd taken centuries alone and traveling across multiple continents, but the fates had tracked him down and thrown her right into his path at just the right moment. There was no denying her, no hiding from her, no avoiding. She was his and he was hers.

And he felt buried in the need to prove it to everyone. Phego wanted to drag Michaela back to the barn and lick every curve of her body, needed to hear her scream his name and beg for more. He craved her release, was dying to give her everything she desired. Hell, he'd bury himself inside of her and exchange mating bites right there on the bloodied grass if that was what she asked for. Anything for her, everything for her. All because of her.

Hell, he wanted to make sure every male knew she was the mate of a warrior who wouldn't stop to think before castrating him if he even thought of looking at her sideways. But once again, he was interrupted.

"I hate to break up your mating stuff," Ariel said, clutching her stomach and curling over in pain. "But this baby's still coming soon. I sort of need Michaela."

Phego growled and pulled away, squeezing Michaela's ass for good measure before dropping his arms. She didn't go easily, though. Thank God.

"Time to go to work," Michaela whispered against his lips, holding him in place by the neck. "We'll pick this up later."

And they would. They had time. Lots and lots of time to get to know each other, to fall in love with one another, and to simply be mated. Phego was looking forward to it.

He kissed her sugar-sweet lips one last time before letting her go so she could do what she'd come for. And so he could watch her ass swing under her thin skirt. Michaela was halfway up the steps when Thaus came racing around the corner of the cabin. Phego jumped to the bottom of the porch, ready to defend, ready to keep his mate safe even if it was from his own brother.

The one who had eyes for no one but his mate.

"What the fuck? Why is there a dead wolf back here?" He headed straight for Ariel, not waiting for an answer. Not needing one quite yet, apparently. But Ariel refused to wait for him. She was already in motion when Thaus hit the stairs, which gave Phego the chance to pull his own mate back into his arms. Just to keep her out of Thaus' way, of course.

"You made it," Ariel said as Thaus picked her up off the ground. Michaela sighed and cuddled closer to Phego, resting her head on his shoulder. Watching the other couple as Phego watched her.

"Told you I would." Thaus kissed Ariel quickly, the two pressed together in a way that seemed almost impossible considering her shape at that moment. "But really, why is there a dead wolf back here?"

"It's been a long couple of days." Deus clapped Thaus on the back. "I'll take care of the dead wolf here and the body of Colt out front. You all can deal with that baby."

Thaus' eyes went wide, and he whipped his head back to gape at Ariel. "You're in labor?"

She grinned. "Yeah. Are you ready to be a daddy?"

Thaus shot a look at Phego that could only be described as panicked before licking his lips and giving his mate a nod. "Yes. Of course. But, hang on. What body out front?"

Ariel looked ready to push him back off the porch. "Seriously? That's what you're worried about right now?"

Thaus shrugged. "Dead things, angel. There are dead things. Or, well, dead thing. Dead wolf. Singular."

Phego grinned down at Michaela as she shook with restrained laughter in his arms.

"Behave," he whispered to her.

"I'm trying, but they're cute together."

Phego had to agree. He also had to explain to Thaus about the bodies. The dead ones. "There's a body of a man named Colt out front at the tree line. Or at least, what's left of him."

Thaus growled. "No, there isn't. I came around that way."

The group froze for about half a second before Phego set Michaela on her feet and took off at a run toward the front yard. But when he got there, Thaus and Deus following right behind him, there was no body. No Colt.

"Fuck," he hissed, staring down at the blood-soaked piece of grass where the fucker should have been. "He was dead."

"I know," Michaela said, coming up behind him. "I'm sure of it."

"No way he survived that," Deus replied. "I'll search for...whatever I can find."

"Uh, guys?" Ariel said, panting through her clenched teeth. "I hate to interrupt—"

"No interruptions. It's just time to deliver a baby." Michaela took a step toward Ariel, but before she could pull away, Phego tugged her closer, twisted her around, and rested his forehead against hers.

Time to lay everything out on the line. "You can't go back to your pack."

Michaela frowned. "Why not?"

"Was Colt working with Gressil?"

Her eyes widened, and her brow tightened into a furrow. "I don't know. I...don't think so, but I can't be sure. I certainly hope not."

Just as he'd expected. "Hope's not enough. I need you safe, and I have to be sure. I don't trust your pack."

"You don't trust anyone."

Phego couldn't deny that. Well, maybe… He caught Deus looking his way, and then he checked on Thaus, was stood on the porch with Ariel in his arms. His brothers were watching. Monitoring. Making sure everyone was safe. His brothers. His true family.

"I trust my Dire pack," Phego said. "No one else."

Michaela's face fell, but Phego was ready for that. He tucked a finger under her chin and tilted her face to his. Refusing to let her avoid his eyes as he professed his truth.

"No one but them and you. You're part of the pack now."

Her smile spread slowly, lighting up her eyes like the sun creeping over the mountains. "Really?"

"Really. You're mine." He gave her a soft kiss on the lips, a promise of sorts, before pulling back and looking her square in the eye once more. "And I'm not trying to be unreasonable, but you can't ever go back to your old pack. Not after this."

Michaela stared at him, investigating something. Looking for more than he knew how to give. "Never?"

Guilt had him sighing. "Maybe someday, if we ever figure out what happened to Colt and how he was involved with Gressil, if at all. But for now…"

He couldn't say it. Too afraid she'd back away. That she'd leave. That she'd find the possibility of a life with him less appealing than returning to her friends and family.

But Michaela surprised him with a quiet, "Fine."

"Fine?"

"Yes, fine. Hopefully, I can go back at some point. I'd like to see my family again. But for now, we can avoid them. I felt comfortable when we came here, so maybe this was meant to be."

Phego just shook his head, dread a heavy knot in his gut. "We can't stay here, either."

"Why not?"

"Colt knows where we live."

Michaela frowned again. "What if Deus finds him... his body?"

"He could have sent word to others. Someone could know where you are right now. I wouldn't feel comfortable with you anywhere near these woods. I wouldn't be able to know you were safe."

It took her far longer to nod than he would have liked. "So we have to move?"

Phego could only offer her the truth. "Yes."

"Together?"

As if there was another option. "Yes."

"Fine." She rose up on the balls of her feet to press her lips to his before pulling away and catching his gaze. "So long as we're together, I'll go where you do. The fates brought us together. Who am I to try to tear us apart?"

And that was it. Those words, that acceptance, was all he needed. She was his, he was hers, and they were headed off soon to start a new life together. He'd drag her out of the woods right at that moment if it weren't for Ariel.

Michaela was on the porch and helping the woman of the hour inside when Phego yelled out to her again. "How long until Ariel can be moved?"

Thaus growled. "Fuck, man. She's having a baby."

"Three days, minimum," Michaela said, ignoring Thaus' crankiness.

"We leave in three days, then."

Michaela waved her acceptance of his words and disappeared inside, Thaus right behind her. Phego took a moment to catch his breath, to let his wolf senses spread and get a feel for the earth around him. He'd have to be on guard, watching over the Omegas every second as they waited out Ariel's recovery. Thaus would be on board the second he understood what had happened. Hell, he'd probably try to figure out a way to remove Ariel from danger before she'd had those three days.

Deus sidled up beside him, looking frustrated and worried. "Nothing. Scent trail ends at the fucking creek."

"Same trick as Gressil."

"Yup." Deus sighed and ran a hand over his short hair. "I swear, that man was dead. There was no way he could have survived that attack."

"Did you scent anyone else on the trail?"

"No."

"Then he survived. Somehow, he lived through Gressil's attack and got away from us."

"Fuck," Deus hissed. "What do you want to do?"

"Kill the bastard for being a threat to my mate, but that will have to wait." Phego's lip curled, though the snarl he wanted to issue stayed silent. That backstabbing motherfucker. "Three days for Ariel and the baby to heal, then Michaela and I need to disappear."

"Understood."

But Phego wasn't sure he did. "She's my mate. If they find her...if they know where she is..."

Deus looked right at him, his eyes solid. His words sure and strong. "It'll be as if she never existed."

"Good," Phego said, relief easing the tightness in his shoulders. "Stay on it. And cover the front while they're inside. I'll take the back."

Deus grunted and turned, but not before giving Phego one last shot. "You're not going to go inside and watch the beauty of a new life being brought into the world?"

"Not until it's mine." Phego shifted and raced toward the back of the house, ready to defend his mate. Ready to destroy any threat to her.

Ready to give his heart to a woman for the first and last time of his life.

Epilogue

The seaside cabin sat on the edge of a grass-covered cliff, the building small and quaint in that way mostly only seen in movies. Michaela had come to love the old, charming building. The matching one a hundred yards away at the edge of the woods was just as cute, even more so with its gray cedar shingles and deep blue trim. But that cabin, the one that was usually home to her and Phego, sat empty. Michaela's mate had been pulled away on a mission, and the silence of her home was too much to bear some days. Which was why she sat at Ariel's cabin watching the waves crash against the rocks farther down the coast and rocking the bassinet of a tiny wolf shifter she'd help bring into the world.

That and the fact that Phego had made her move in with Ariel, Thaus, and the baby while he was gone.

"What time will they be back?" Ariel asked as she ripped open another box.

Michaela turned away from the window and grabbed

the last of the books off the counter, heading to the bookshelf in the corner. "Soon. Phego promised he'd be here before sunset."

"And if he's late?"

"He won't be." Michaela smiled as Ariel laughed, both knowing exactly how true those words were. Being late wouldn't happen. Her mate had made her a promise, and if there was one thing Michaela had learned about him in the two months they'd been mated, it was that Phego didn't break his word. Ever. He was the most trustworthy person she'd ever met.

Ariel stopped by the bassinet in the corner to tuck a blanket around her sleeping son before crossing back to the stack of boxes they were going through. Moving sucked—it sucked more with a newborn in tow. Unpacking had taken both couples far longer than they'd planned, though not for the same reasons. Michaela didn't have a little baby to watch over.

She had a mate who couldn't keep his hands, mouth, and cock to himself. Thank the fates for that. Four days without his touch was too much. She wanted him home. Immediately.

"I can't believe he had a mission so soon," Ariel said as she reached to set a book on a high shelf.

"He's investigating the possibility of more Dire Wolves with Deus. It wasn't so much a mission, more of a recon thing," Thaus said as he slipped into the room from the back door. Ariel squeaked and dropped the book, running toward her mate as if she hadn't seen him less than an hour before. Thaus met her in the middle of the room, the two grinning and coming together in an embrace that was just this side of PG-rated. Michaela didn't mind, though. She was sure she and Phego were the same. Or they would be once he made it home to her.

"Recon schmechon," Michaela said, turning her back on

the couple to place a few more books on the shelves. "Luc called and told him to go do stuff. Therefore, it's a mission. One I can't wait to be over so I can have Phego back with me."

Thaus chuckled. "You sick of staying with us already?"

"Yes." Michaela turned and grinned, softening her words. "But only because I want my mate with me in our little home. Plus, you three deserve your privacy."

The buzz of his phone had Thaus looking down, distracted. "Yeah, well, we appreciate that, but Phego would kill me if I let anything happen to you. You're stuck with us until this is over."

"I know," Michaela said with a sigh. "I just miss him, I guess."

"Well, you won't have to miss him for long." Thaus tucked his phone back into his pocket. "They've crossed the state line."

Michaela grinned, practically bouncing on her toes. "How far is that from here?"

"An hour...maybe." He growled and grabbed Ariel again, rocking her back and forth. "Though if he's anything like me after a mission, he'll be hauling ass to get to his mate, so it could be less."

Michaela dropped the last of the books on the shelf and headed for the door. "Gotta go. I want to take a shower before he gets here."

Thaus laughed. "He won't care if you're dirty."

"Maybe not, but I will," Michaela called just before she raced outside. Before she could make it back to her cabin, before she could even cross the field between the two, she spotted the shadow of a wolf on the far hill running toward their little cliffside homes.

And running fast.

Michaela shivered, arousal blooming within her. She knew that shape, sensed her mate, felt the connection between them pull tight as she watched the beast running full tilt for her. Phego was home.

As the sun turned the sky cotton-candy pink, Phego's wolf hit the edge of their property. Michaela waited, anxious but nervous, too. Needful but trying to hold herself back. Phego shifted human once he was about ten yards away, running right to Michaela and picking her up in his arms as he hurried toward the cabin.

"You could have walked," Michaela said, though the way she clung to him, the way she wrapped her body around his, belied her words. She hadn't wanted him to walk. Hell, anything to get him home faster. Thankfully, he understood.

"And miss an extra minute with you?" Phego yanked on her shirt as they crossed the threshold into their house, ripping the fabric in two before moving his hands to tug her skirt from her body. "Not a chance."

Michaela helped him rid her of her clothes, thankful he was already naked. "I'm glad you're early. I missed you."

"Missed you more." Phego bit her neck, a reminder of the mating mark there. As always, he continued licking, kissing, and sucking along her shoulder to the spot where his claw marks glowed pale against her dark skin. It was his way of apologizing, his penance for hurting her, he liked to say. She didn't care about the marks. She just wanted him touching her.

"I was going to shower," she said, moaning as he rubbed a knuckle against her clit. She was so wet, so ready for him.

Phego grunted and lifted her back into his arms. "I like you dirty."

Michaela chuckled, tightening her legs around his hips and rocking her hips so she could rub against his cock. So she could be the one to tease him for once. "Any trouble while you were gone?"

Phego groaned, spinning to press her back against a wall and dragging his cock along her pussy. Bumping her clit on every pass and grinning when she jerked. "None. You?"

Michaela shook her head, sighing when he finally thrust inside. "Fuck, I needed this. Needed you."

"I know, baby. I can feel it. You're so fucking wet for me." Phego pushed harder, slid deeper. Pressing her into the wall with every thrust. "Thaus keep an eye on you?"

How he could keep up such a conversation, she had no idea. "Yes, but his aren't the eyes I want looking my way."

Phego growled, pinching her nipple as he held her ass in one hand. "No?"

"No." Michaela bumped her head against the wall as he grew more wild. As he grunted through every push, slamming her hips into the wall. As he lost control and gave her what she wanted. "Fuck, I need to come."

"I know, mate. I feel it." He slid his hand between them, pressing his thumb against her clit as he filled her over and over again. "We need a bed. Did we get a bed while I was gone?"

"Yes," she hissed, so close to coming she could barely find her words. "It's here, but I haven't slept in it yet."

He snarled and pulled her away from the wall, carrying her into their bedroom where a perfectly huge, pristinely made white bed took up most of the space.

"Nice," he said as he laid her out before him. "I want to fuck you in our bed."

"Come," she said, pulling him down on top of her, spreading her legs wide so he could slide back inside as she sank into the bedding. "Come inside me, mate. I want to feel you. I want to be yours."

Phego plowed her into the mattress, losing all rhythm as he snarled and snapped at her neck. That was Michaela's favorite side to her mate, the animalistic one. The out of control lover who would do anything for his mate. The side no one but she ever got to see.

Her Phego.

The state they lived in didn't matter, the house they chose didn't either. So long as they were together, so long as she could feel his skin against hers and taste his kiss, they'd be okay. No matter how many Dire Wolves were out in the world. She was safe with her mate, and he was safe with her. Always.

A *Dire Wolves* MISSION

Coming soon from *USA Today*
bestselling author
Ellis Leigh

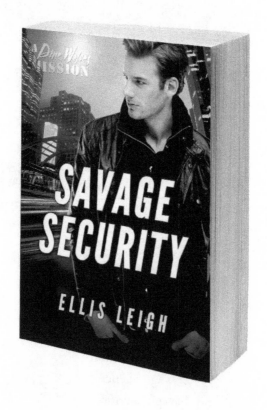

A *Dire Wolves* MISSION

Also
Available

FERAL BREED MOTORCYCLE CLUB
Claiming His Fate
Claiming His Need
Claiming His Witch
Claiming His Beauty
Claiming His Fire
Claiming His Desire

FERAL BREED FOLLOWINGS
Claiming His Chance
Claiming His Prize
Claiming His Grace

THE GATHERING
Killian & Lyra
Gideon & Kalie
Blasius, Dante, & Moira
Blasius, Dante, & Moira: Homecoming

About
the Author

A storyteller from the time she could talk, *USA Today* bestsellng author Ellis Leigh grew up among family legends of hauntings, psychics, and love spanning decades. Those stories didn't always have the happiest of endings, so they inspired her to write about real life, real love, and the difficulties therein. From farmers to werewolves, store clerks to witches—if there's love to be found, she'll write about it. Ellis lives in the Chicago area with her husband, daughters, and to tiny fish that take up way too much of her time.

www.ellisleigh.com

9 781944 336202